DECAY

A ZOMBIE STORY

DECAY

A ZOMBIE STORY

JOSEPH DUMAS

In memory of Bill Gorman.
Bill, you really helped me while I was originally
developing Decay and gave me the confidence
to move forward with it. I miss you, buddy,
Rest in Peace.

DECAY: A ZOMBIE STORY
Copyright © 2011 Open Casket Press
ISBN Softcover ISBN 13: 978-1-61199-041-6   ISBN 10: 1-611990-41-6
All rights reserved.
Open Casket Press is an imprint of Living Dead Press.
ww.livingdeadpress.com
For more info on obtaining additional copies of this book, contact:
www.opencasketpress.com
Edited by Kevin Lewis

THE END BEGINS

PETER

It was a beautiful day, a true beginning to the summer season, and a true end of another school year. I had just arrived home from running errands, trying to find a place to fix the radio in my car. It hadn't been working right since the battery died months ago. Unfortunately, the place I went to, which was hours away, had unexpectedly closed for the day; a family emergency perhaps.

After I got out of my car, I began walking to the house, a yellow suburban home in Massachusetts. While approaching the door, I was greeted by the joyful barks of my mom's dog, Fido, a small German shepherd puppy. Next, my cell phone rang and I answered it as I entered the house.

"Hello?"

"Hey, Pete," Jen, my girlfriend, said.

"Hey, sweetie. How's it going?" I asked.

"Good. I'm on my way over. I spoke to Robbie and Sam earlier. They're going to swing by with a movie later on…"

"Oh okay," I said. "But just so you know, even though my mom's out of town, I don't really want to have a huge party…"

"Well, I just invited them and told Sam to tell Robbie it's just going to be a quiet evening…"

"Okay, sorry for getting snappy, it's just, you know… it's Robbie, he doesn't know what *quiet* means," I said.

Excited at the idea of hanging out with our friends Robbie and Samantha for the evening, we finalized our plans and I hung up the phone.

Moments later, there was a knock at the door—it was Jen. As she entered the house, I greeted her with a kiss and a take-out menu. It was a pizza place down the street. We ordered our usual strange combination of one veggie pizza and one 'meat lover's' pizza.

After ordering the food, Jen noticed a note left by my mom on the table. The note instructed me to have someone come and fix the broken window in the laundry room. "Did you do this?" Jen asked as she held up the note.

"No not yet," I explained. "But I did duct tape a trash bag over it to keep any animals out."

"Pete! That's still not safe, get it fixed!"

Jen was pretty paranoid about robbers and home invasions, thanks to watching way too many crime shows. I explained to her that we lived in one of the safest towns in the state and I would get the window fixed on Monday. She angrily accepted this and we walked to the pizza place.

The streets were pretty quiet despite it being rush hour. Upon arriving at the pizza joint, we discovered it was pretty quiet in there as well. The guys working looked pretty bored; they barely noticed when we entered. They were all just standing around watching TV. I didn't mind too much, but Jen was getting frustrated that they didn't acknowledge us. So, after politely getting their attention, we got the pizzas and let them get back to the television.

We left the restaurant and headed back to my house. The streets were still quiet for the most part. Suddenly, we heard a loud screech, and turned around to see a gold station wagon, nearly on two wheels turning onto my street. I threw up my hands as the jerk blew past us, shattering the speed limit for sure. "What the hell is his problem?" I yelled.

"Hopefully he'll get a ticket," Jen said. "There are kids in this area, that's so dangerous!"

A little after we returned to my house, a bright red convertible pulled into my driveway; Robbie was driving with his girlfriend— Jen's best friend, Samantha, or Sam. Robbie and I have been friends since we were kids. Jen and I recently introduced him to Sam, something Jen wasn't too thrilled about in the beginning, since Sam had a difficult upbringing and Robbie always had a drinking problem. Sam's parents died years ago, leaving her to live with her father's single brother, who from what I understand is something of an alcoholic himself. Needless to say, these circumstances have led Jen to be a bit weary of the idea of Robbie being in Sam's life. But to her chagrin, they hit it off and have been together for months now. Robbie also cut down on his drinking habits; something I've been hoping would happen since we began college in '05.

Robbie brought over *The Departed* for us to watch; he can't seem to get enough of this movie.

"Ready for a good flick?" Robbie asked excitedly as he got out of his car.

"Yeah, man, sure," I said.

"Good thing we got here in one piece," Robbie shook his head.

"What happened?"

"Some guy almost killed us!" Samantha said in an overwhelmed tone.

"We saw a station wagon fly by!" Jen said. "Was it the same one?"

They both nodded.

After we finished discussing the wannabe NASCAR driver, we decided to head inside, have some dinner, and watch the movie. I got myself and Jen some beers from the fridge. Sam doesn't drink for obvious reasons, and Robbie turned down the offer altogether.

But the only reason he turned down the offer was because he was hitting his own bottle hard, one he kept hidden in the cargo pocket of his jacket. I was a little worried about him drinking but he didn't seem like he was intending to get drunk, but rather was just maintaining a good buzz.

JEN

The night had been going rather smoothly. Good pizza, good friends, and a decent movie. I'd never seen it before, not bad for the most part. I guess it's ideal for the filmmaker-type-of-viewer, but I was just stuck on the over-exaggerated Boston accents.

However, the seemingly chill night soon became one of tremendous drama. Robbie began swigging down whatever hard liquor was in his secret stash. Soon, Sam told him to stop—or at least slow down, but rather than slow down, he nearly finished the bottle within minutes. He proceeded to get up and start dancing around like something out of Saturday Night Fever.

Next, almost as if his horseplay were scripted, he played the part of a true jackass, and while trying to pull Sam off the couch, he knocked over Pete's mom's favorite lamp, where it then smashed apart on the floor.

Utterly ridiculous! At this point, Pete came running in from the kitchen, where he was cleaning things up.

"What the hell happened?" he screamed as Fido began barking like mad.

"Robbie's drunk," a frightened Sam said, as she had never truly witnessed the drunken mess we know and fear. Further, despite all of this chaos, Robbie continued trying to get Sam to dance with him as he stomped the pieces of broken glass into the low weave carpet.

"Robbie, calm down!" I told him.

"Shut the fuck up, you bitch!" he screamed and slurred back at me without hesitation.

Pete quickly let Fido into the backyard to calm down and said to Robbie, "Whoa man, calm down! You're drunk!"

Then, Robbie's drunken self said, "No way, man, you tell your chick to mind her fuckin' business."

Immediately, Pete grabbed him by his arm and pulled him towards the door. What happened next would change the rest of our lives…

ROBBIE

Everyone's got their issues and vices in life. I like to drink, get drunk, and have a good time. Then, my *friends* try to tell me I'm an alcoholic—fuck that! I'm a college student, well, sort of. I probably won't go back in the fall.

My father owns a chain of hardware stores throughout New England known as 'Fix-It Hardware.' I have an assistant manager position at the original store not far from our neighborhood. I've recently made the decision that I'll take on his duties in the next five or so years when he throws in the towel.

As a matter of fact, while we were watching the movie, my old man called my cell.

"Rob! Get home now!" he told me very calmly.

"Hold up, Dad. Why?" I asked very politely.

"You took the keys to the store with you again! Bring them home now!" he continued telling me.

"Come on, Dad, I'm not exactly fit to operate a motor vehicle right now," I insisted because I truly am responsible.

Next, he continued yelling and cussing into the phone which I'm sure needed some kind of 'drain-O' after the amount of saliva it'd surely just absorbed thanks to the greatest spit-yeller since wrestling legend Sgt. Slaughter.

So, knowing I wasn't going anywhere until the A.M., I kept my drink on and apparently got a little too rowdy. Broke a lamp, I think. Pete and Jen were yelling—hurting my head. And Sam, my girlfriend, she started crying and wouldn't even look at me.

Soon, Pete got fed up with me and brought me outside. He took my keys and told me to get some air and try to sober up a little. After Pete left me outside to stew over my mistakes, some dude in a business suit started stumbling towards me. This guy was definitely wasted or something, mumbling and stumbling all over the place.

I waved him down just to make sure he was all right, because he was making me look like I was blowing a .07 in comparison. Finally, the drunkard made his way down Pete's driveway. As he got closer and into the light, I noticed he looked like he'd been in an accident— he was covered in blood. Needless to say, this helped my sobering up.

"You all right, man?" I asked, standing up from the ground in shame. He continued groaning and mumbling until he reached out and grabbed me with his cold and bloody mitts. Then, I don't know what happened, but his wrinkly, dried-up lips curled around his bloody white teeth and the guy bit me on the neck!

TARA

I arrived at work around 4:30 in the afternoon. The Georgio's Pizza employee parking lot seemed unusually empty. On a Friday that's often a very bad sign. My co-workers probably found some party or event to attend together, leaving me to cover on the busiest night of the week.

As I entered through the back of the building, my phone beeped. My boyfriend sent me a text message: Hey sweetie, don't forget to ask about your birthday. 3 p.m.

I stopped and began messaging him back, but before I could type one word, my boss came storming around the corner.

"Thank God, Tara!" my boss, Paul, shouted at the sight of me. "Claire and Alice both called in sick and we've got a full house out there!"

"Oh jeez," I said. "Who's been waiting tables?"

Paul wiped his forehead with his apron and said, "Me, that's who. And Teddy is the only one in the kitchen, too!"

"What? Really? Where is everyone?"

"Sick I guess. Sounded bad, too. The others…well, I have no idea," Paul said.

The restaurant phone began to ring and Paul started walking to his office.

"And on top of all that," he said while walking away, "our cable's out. No TV in the whole restaurant."

So, the customers had been waiting extra-long with nothing to keep them entertained in the meantime. Thinking about what I was walking into, I realized my tips would be extra-frugal tonight.

I put my things in a locker and started putting on my apron. I then realized I never got back to my boyfriend. Therefore, I decided to keep my phone in my apron pocket.

On the off-chance I got a moment to myself, I would text him back.

As I finished getting ready, I overheard Paul talking on the phone.

"What do you mean you can't send anyone out today? No, I haven't seen the news! I don't have any cable! Huh-Hello? Hello?"

I could almost feel his blood pressure rising from a room away. So, I decided to do what I could and just get out there and help some hungry people.

"Start with Table 28!" Paul shouted to me, as I began walking away.

PETER

"Pete! Help! Help! Peter! Samantha! Someone!"

The yelling came from outside. Robbie was in some kind of trouble it seemed, but knowing his state of mind, he could be running from a daddy-long-leg, or even his own shadow. Nonetheless, I immediately went out there to see. What I came across would become ingrained in my brain forever.

A decrepit businessman had tackled Robbie on the steps. Blood was everywhere. The haggard man lashed at Robbie, snapping his teeth like some kind of pissed-off rabid animal. As soon as I got out there, Robbie jabbed his attacker with a hard right to the jaw. Teeth flew from the man's mouth and Robbie struggled to his feet as blood gushed from the side of his neck.

The sickly man struggled to get back on his feet and back to us for whatever reason. I pushed Robbie towards the door to get him inside. Then, I pushed the man back further away from the house. As I turned to follow Robbie back inside, someone grabbed me by the shoulder. Startled nearly to death, I tripped over myself and fell to the ground. This other person, an older man, possibly homeless, grabbed at my feet and—I think—bit into my shoe, though I didn't really feel anything through the rugged leather. Then I gave him a further taste as I booted him away from me. Robbie and I got to the door and created a somewhat safe distance from these people.

I looked down the street and saw a few more people stumbling in our general direction. I began wondering exactly what the hell was going on. Then, as I was about to open the door, I looked at Robbie. His eyes were rolling back into his head, and he began coughing up blood and losing his balance. Within a flash of a second, he fell over the porch railing and seemed to stop breathing. At the same time, the drunk - sick, or whatever people, crowded onto the front lawn.

Next, Robbie began moving around. Relieved and confused, I grabbed him by the arm and told him we had to get inside. He shook his head and began mumbling incoherently. After a second, he lifted his head and lunged at me. His eyes, they looked different now, not like Robbie's normal eyes, more like something dead or missing, something bloody and dangerous. While lunging at me, he snapped his teeth and bit the collar of my polo shirt. I pushed him away like I had the other people. His neck wound appeared to have stopped bleeding and the blood was no longer gushing from his mouth. But it was his eyes. I could see Robbie wasn't in there anymore, and what remained was nothing but hunger. I shoved him away from me, ran inside, and locked the door behind me.

Jen and Sam stared at me and my blood-spattered clothing. Before I could tell them what had happened to Robbie and the crazy people outside, I saw that the news was on the television, and they seemed somewhat hypnotized by the broadcast. I looked on as one of the less recognized anchors sat there with a blank look on his face, reporting what sounded more like an excerpt from a Stephen King novel or the movie-of-the-week.

"For those just tuning in, an epidemic has swept the entire East coast, as well as the Great Lakes Region of the United States. This disease, or virus, is highly contagious," he explained. "We highly suggest avoiding any and all close contact with those infected with the virus as it spreads rapidly through bite wounds, scratches, and other close contact."

Immediately, I knew what happened to Robbie and what could have happened to me. I stared at the television for a moment and could hear the muffled frantic voices of Sam and Jen in the background.

"What happened?"

"Is Robbie okay?"

"Where's Robbie?"

"Are you okay?"

Then, the anchor said, "We repeat, the virus is known to spread through bite wounds..."

A tear ran down my cheek as I realized I may have just lost my best friend. Samantha stood up and looked at me.

"Robbie?" she asked nervously.

I shook my head no and looked down at my feet. Samantha began crying.

MIKE

Rush hour traffic had decided to stick around for a couple more hours as I sat and stared into space on the Mass Pike. I was returning from the 'Annual Bike-A-thon' in New Jersey, where I placed 3rd for the second year in a row. I've just hit the thirty year milestone in life and am beginning to realize that I can't go like I used to. It's getting hard to keep up with the up-and-coming new kids.

I was stuck in bumper-to-bumper traffic in the most inconvenient spot possible, as I was transitioning from one radio station feed to the next. Zeppelin was cutting in and out on one and *Bye Bye Miss American Pie* had begun to chime in on the other.

Soon, I gave up and made the switch from FM to AM; if only I'd listened to my ex and invested in one of the satellite radios—or even a damn CD player. My car was crap. Nevertheless, I began flipping through the unfamiliarity of AM radio. I had gotten some Beethoven, maybe Mozart or Bach; couldn't really tell. Next up was what sounded like a Red Sox broadcast from the early '90s being rebroadcast. I soon settled on a local news station, being hosted by what sounded to be your stereotypical conspiracy theorist broadcasting out of an illegally parked RV somewhere in a dirt lot.

"The government wants you to believe a sickness is running rampant. They want you to believe the end has come. They want you to run and spend money on those necessities; the ones at CVS funded by government officials and sponsoring our own Senator!"

"Is this guy okay?" I pondered aloud.

"Furthermore, I wouldn't be the least bit surprised to learn that the government themselves has been releasing some kind of toxin into the air, just to wipe some of us out, control the population a little. I mean, do they really expect us to believe they can't cure cancer or AIDS! Cow poop, my friends, if they can put a man on the moon, they can cure these illnesses. Speaking of that, we all know the moon landing was Hollywood's biggest project and never really..."

I decided to exercise one of my freedoms by shutting off the radio. I never thought a traffic jam would seem so peaceful and quiet regardless of the beeping and shouting. Suddenly, the car behind me jerked forward and slammed into my bumper. Furious, I unbuckled my seatbelt to go get this person's information. As I was about to open my door, the driver in the car behind me got out and ran past me frantically.

I sat back in my seat and looked into my rearview mirror. Some people—two men and a woman—began to pull an older gentleman out of his car and began ruthlessly attacking him. I then looked at the cars next to me and noticed they were empty. As I continued observing my surroundings, I noticed this was the case in many cars.

Next, I saw a couple of bloody people stumbling between cars behind me. Not knowing exactly what to do, I made an executive decision and grabbed the photo of my daughter, Ellie, off the dash. Then, I quickly got out of my car and removed my bike from the roof rack.

I hopped on and began cruising through the stalled traffic, past people screaming, crying, and I think some were even biting each other.

I passed several abandoned cars; some had crashed and had caught fire. I did my best to maintain a steady and safe speed throughout whatever I was seeing. However, as I continued my path through the wreckage, I soon was forced to swerve out of the way of a door flying open and someone calling out for help.

I looked back for a moment, unsure of what to do, and drove my bicycle off the road and into the woods. I began riding uncontrollably through a downhill slope of trees, logs, and weeds. Soon enough, my front tire stopped dead when it smashed into a large, fallen tree. I was sent flying through the air with nothing to stop my fall.

PETER

Samantha had gone into the bathroom with Jen to try and get a hold of herself. Soon, Jen returned and we scoped out the front yard together; several of these evidently sick people still stumbled around the front steps. However, there was no sign of Robbie anywhere.

As I began trying to gather my thoughts and figure out exactly what the hell was happening, Fido scurried into the room. At first, I didn't think anything of it, but I soon realized I had let Fido into the backyard. No one let him back in. So, that means I left the door open or one of those things opened it. Either way, I didn't feel too safe knowing the house wasn't secure.

As I turned to check the back door, I noticed that I'd likely left it wide open during all the commotion. That being said, two sickly strangers were stumbling up the steps. I dashed to the door and literally slammed it in their faces. Relieved that the house might in fact be secure, I began trying once again to gather my thoughts and form a plan. Not that I thought it would help, I told Jen to call 9-1-1. She dialed and got a busy signal. So it looked like this wasn't an isolated incident; as if the news broadcasts weren't enough evidence of that.

Next, our problems continued to build when a loud crash came from the laundry room. Jen grabbed Fido and brought him to the bathroom to stay with Sam. I went to my room and grabbed a Louisville Slugger, and then continued to the laundry room, hoping and praying that my mom had gotten a cat while I was away at school and it just knocked something over.

I slowly opened the door. Ambient light shone into the room, revealing the trash bag that once covered the broken window, lying on the floor—not good. I began to accept the fact that this wasn't the work of an unknown house cat, especially when I saw Robbie coming around a dark corner. His face looked very sickly and pale, his eyes dark and dead. His body was beaten and bloody; it looked like something straight out of a zombie movie.

"Robbie," I said to him.

He grunted something, semi-acknowledging my voice. He began to come towards me in a very threatening fashion. I gripped the bat and almost swung at him. However, at the last minute, I decided to run. I couldn't take a baseball bat to my best friend, regardless of his current state-of-mind.

I shut the door and slid my mom's ironing board in front of it to barricade him in. I then ran to the bathroom and opened the door. Sam, Jen and Fido were sitting on the edge of the tub, scared and unsure of what to do.

"We're leaving," I insisted.

With no other ideas, they stood up and followed me to the front door. Before we headed to the car, I took a peek outside; the yard seemed to have cleared up. Without any more hesitation, I opened the door and told everyone to run to my car.

But as we got to the car, I tried to unlock it, realizing that I had Robbie's keys—not mine.

"Shit!" I shouted to myself.

Suddenly, the same fellows from the backyard began coming around the fence.

"Robbie's car! Go to Robbie's car!" I told them.

I unlocked the car and we were off. Jen asked me what the plan was, and during the chaotic exit, I remembered Robbie's phone conversation with his dad, and how he had the keys to the hardware store in his car. Immediately, I told Jen to take a look around. She found the key ring in the messy glove compartment and we continued on our now apparent path to the hardware store.

KELLY

I couldn't believe the things that were happening. It was about two hours ago at my apartment, the Super came to collect rent—I was running a little late, but he's an asshole anyways—or should I say he *was* an asshole. When he came into my place, his arm was all bandaged up. He told me he had been mugged earlier that day.

I didn't know what to think, nor did I really care until he collapsed in the middle of my kitchen. I wasn't about to give him CPR, but I didn't wish death upon him either—regardless of him being a prick. So, I did what anyone would've done, I called 9-1-1. There was a busy tone, a busy tone! So, I proceeded downstairs to the Mikesons, where I found an open door and a seemingly empty apartment. I didn't know what was going on, so I went back to check on the Super—he was… gone?

Part of me was glad he was okay, but part of me was wondering what the hell was going on in my building. I sat down at the table, trying to piece everything together when I heard a noise from the other room, someone walking around. It must have been the Super.

I went to check it out, and I saw him stumbling slowly around my living room.

"Are you okay?" I asked. "You were out for a minute there."

He turned around with a blank look on his face and began coming towards me, stumbling around and into the coffee table and tripping over himself.

"Sir, are you okay?" I asked again.

With no response, I began backing out of the room. I got a good look at his face and realized that no one seemed to be home.

"I'm not paying my rent," I said nervously. If this wouldn't warrant a reaction, nothing would.

He maintained his pace, stumbling towards me, reaching and grunting.

At this point, I ran through the kitchen and made it to the pantry, where I reached for my hidden weapon, a solid shotgun and a small box of shells. As I reached for the box, I knocked it off the shelf, spilling them all over the kitchen. I grabbed a couple quickly, well aware there was one ready to go in the chamber— what's the point in having a shotgun if it isn't ready to go?

I cocked the shotgun, pointed it at the Super and shouted, "Stay back or I'll shoot!" He continued to lurch towards me and suddenly slipped on one of the scattered shotgun shells, falling face first towards me. Before I could react, he'd fallen into me and we landed with me on the bottom! I slid out from underneath his large beer belly and rolled over the shell and tile kitchen floor; all the while he's trying to bite me, the sick fuck.

As I made it to my feet, he reached for me, grunted loudly—almost yelling. I reached down and grabbed another handful of shells and shoved them in my pocket. At this point, I turned around, leaving my apartment and my Super. I closed the door, hoping he wouldn't follow me.

When I was outside, I looked for anyone that could help me. Eventually, I came across a police car, parked behind a sign for burgers on the road; probably trying to catch speeders. I ran to the car, putting my shotgun down along the way—knowing the cop would probably blow my brains out all over the road if I approached him with it.

"Officer, please!" I shouted as I ran around to the driver's side, only to find the door ajar and an empty vehicle. I saw the walkie-talkie sitting in the center console and immediately grabbed it and held down the long button on the side, hoping it was the right one.

"Hello? Is anyone there? Hello?"

I released the button and listened for a moment—static, nothing more. At this point, I realized that something had to have happened; maybe the Super wasn't just mugged. I looked up to a dragging sound only to find the cop that likely belonged to the car. He was covered in blood and dragged his right foot as he came my way, grunting in a similar way the Super did.

I'm not a second chance type of girl; so needless to say, I didn't stick around to see if the cop was friendly. I took off running, picked up my shotgun, and headed to the woods.

16

Wearing mostly black, now that night had fallen, I'm pretty sure nothing could see me out here. I sat down on a little rock somewhere near the highway and spotted headlights up the hill, though I'm willing to bet the cars will be in similar shape to the squad car—abandoned, maybe wrecked.

For some reason, I kept thinking back to a religious protester from the Westboro Baptist Church group years ago. He said that the world was ending soon and that God would leave me behind because I've apparently made all of the wrong choices in life. I don't know why this popped into my head.

I never took those people seriously, nor did I care what they think. I guess this whole situation seemed a little surreal and I was just picking it out of my subconscious as some kind of coincidence. Still, I couldn't help but think that I was left behind, and the thought scared me. Not enough to change who I am though.

Suddenly, I heard the rustling and crunching of dead leaves not far behind me in the distance.

I looked up and saw someone silhouetted against the lights from the highway, barreling down the hill. Shortly after, the chaotic rustling stopped and I heard a loud thud, followed by what seemed to be complete silence.

After a moment, I approached where the sound came from. I held my shotgun up, ready to fire. Suddenly, I came across a man, probably around my age, maybe a little older, laying on the ground. He seemed to be knocked out cold.

Laying a mere few feet away was a bicycle with a heavily-warped front tire. I deduced he was probably thrown from the bike and knocked out when his head hit a rock. I don't know why, but part of me wanted to just walk away after everything I'd seen so far, but I decided to stay. I took a seat on a moss-covered lawn and waited for the man to wake up.

TARA

I went out to the restaurant floor; people at two tables were getting up and leaving somewhat frantically while three other tables were already empty. After avoiding the hungry and angry runaways, I went to Table 28 and greeted a sweaty, portly, middle-aged man.

"Welcome to Georgio's, sir, I'm Tara. I'll be your host this evening."

Instead of responding, the man looked down at the table. He began swaying slowly and randomly in his seat. Unsure if something was wrong or if he was just annoyed and trying to decide what to eat; I tried to gain his attention.

"Do you need another moment to decide, sir?" I asked while subtly waving at him.

He started coughing and spat up blood all over his menu and the table. I stared at him for a moment, confused. Then I looked around at the other tables still occupied with customers. They were all staring at the sickly man and whispering at one another.

"Are you all right, sir?" I finally asked.

Suddenly, he fell right out of his chair to the restaurant floor!

"Paul!" I shouted and looked around at the customers as several of them gasped and stood up.

"I'm calling 9-1-1!" shouted a man at another table.

Paul came running out as Teddy watched from the kitchen doors.

"What happened?" Paul shouted and knelt down next to the man. "Tara!" he shouted again.

"Sorry," I said. "I…I don't know, he just fell. He threw up. I think he spit up some blood maybe. He's not well." I was frantic; I didn't know what to do. But Paul did. "Okay, Tara, calm down. Go in the back and get the first aid kit. Hurry," he said.

I was unable to move. Then, out of nowhere, the seemingly disease-ridden man's eyes opened. He got to his feet and bit Paul's neck! He took a chunk right out of his throat!

Paul fell to the side, screaming. Then, as customers began running to the nearest exit, the man started grunting—or moaning—and staring at me. Without giving it a second thought, I ran to the back of the restaurant. I ran past Teddy and to the coat racks, to retrieve my keys from my jacket.

"Hold up, man!" Teddy shouted to the sick man.

I heard a gargling scream and looked back. The man had tackled Teddy and was biting him, too. I could hear yelling from the dining room, the customers probably.

The man left Teddy alone as he bled out on the floor and turned to face me. I was trapped in the hallway, with Teddy dying on the floor and this man stumbling towards me. I did the only thing I could and ran to the walk-in refrigerator. Immediately after going inside, I jammed the door handle with a broomstick.

Then, with the screams softened but still audible, I sat down on a box of processed shredded cheese and cried.

MIKE

I opened my eyes slowly; the unfamiliar surroundings were fuzzy and dark. I moved my head around and heard the crunching sound of dead leaves beneath me. Once my eyes began to focus, I saw a silhouetted figure, a woman, standing over me, holding something.

"Get up," I vaguely heard her say. "Get up."

As I tried to stand up, I focused in on her. She was a young woman with short hair, dark clothes, and, most importantly, was wielding a shotgun.

"Who are you?" I asked with barely enough strength to get the words out.

It had become dark since I took my nap on the forest floor and I couldn't see her face.

"I'm Kelly," she said and extended her hand to me. She helped me up and smiled at me. "I'm glad you're okay," she said. "And not one of *them*."

I assumed she was talking about the people on the highway, the sick people. However, I didn't know what to say to the comment, so I simply began the slow and painful process of getting to my feet. Scared that I might have broken something, I braced myself with my arms—bad idea. Turns out, I dislocated my right shoulder. As I tried to pick myself up, I fell flat on my face and ended up with a mouthful of those wonderfully crunchy and decayed leaves.

Kelly helped me up, and having dealt with the same injury before in my tenure of racing, I showed her what to do, and she popped my shoulder back in place. I'm getting older now and the injury would likely cause me some lagging pain, probably for a few weeks.

We made our way out of the woods quietly and tried to find somewhere safe from this chaotic nightmare. She led the way. While we walked, we told each other what we knew, which wasn't much. I told her what I saw on the highway and briefly heard on the radio.

Then she told me she thought it was a virus of some kind, a sickness that had spread through the area making people lose control. We both thought of terrorists, maybe something biological. That would explain the erratic behavior exhibited by the people on the highway.

She seemed as confused as I was throughout all of this, but kept her cool. Soon enough, we came across a car that had smashed into a street lamp on the edge of the forest opposite the highway. There was no driver in sight. The keys were still in the ignition, and a deflated airbag was on the driver's seat. There was no blood. Perhaps the person had gotten away? There was no way to know.

Kelly and I surveyed the area but it was devoid of life. We made a decision to see if there was a phone or anything in the car. We both looked but were unsuccessful. I didn't have one and Kelly didn't have a phone either—she apparently left her apartment in a hurry.

She turned on the radio to see if we could find out what was going on. She was right; a virus of some kind had swept across most of the country. The reports seemed sketchy, and we sat there in silence, listening anxiously as the broadcaster spoke about the disease and rabid tendencies of those infected, such as biting and scratching—things you'd expect from the Sci-fi movie of the week. Safe-zones had been set up around New England—Massachusetts and New Hampshire mostly.

"And the end begins…" Kelly said softly with a blank look on her face.

PETER

I drove Robbie's car through town, using complete tunnel vision, not seeing or hearing anything around me. I barely remember most of the ride. Jen, Sam, and Fido were whimpering and crying in the back seat. I didn't even have it in me to try and comfort them.

I remember shapes moving along the road and people reaching for the car as we drove through town. Then, I suddenly snapped out of it and began taking in my surroundings when we were closer to the hardware store. Turning the corner, I found myself driving straight for a guy stumbling through the street.

"Pete!" Jen screamed when she saw the man.

I swerved out of the way, hitting the curb and steering the car sideways into a telephone pole. Suddenly, we were upside down in Robbie's car. I was okay and Jen and Fido seemed to be fine as well. Samantha, however, lost consciousness when she hit her head on the window.

My window had shattered in the crash, so I unbuckled myself and began to crawl out of the car. Other than a few scrapes, I was unhurt.

"I'm gonna get you out of there," I told Jen. "Just hold on."

"Okay, I've got Fido," she said. "You need to get Sam out of here first."

As I got to my feet, I saw the man I almost hit stumbling towards us. The thing was, though, he wasn't a man. Well, not anymore. He was one of them now. It made me wonder if it would've even mattered if I'd just hit him and kept on going. The disturbing thought was probably the first time I realized exactly how messed up things were.

Luckily, the back windows were also smashed. I quickly grabbed Fido from Jen and she crawled out of the car, her hands landing on the small shards of safety glass.

I glanced in at Sam, slightly bloody on one side of her face. It didn't look like she was buckled in.

"Sam?" I said, curious if she would respond. As I expected, she didn't. She remained motionless, and if it wasn't for the very slight up-and-down movement of her chest, I would've assumed she was dead.

Suddenly I heard growling—I looked up to see Fido fidgeting in Jen's arms, growling at the monster of a man stumbling towards us.

"Jen, get to the hardware store!" I shouted.

"What about you?"

"Don't worry about me! Get to the store and lock yourself in!" I told her.

Reluctantly, Jen pulled the keys from her pocket and ran across the road to our hopeful safe haven. As she ran around the man, his lifeless eyes followed her every step.

I watched her closely as she easily outran him. Fido's growling and barking seemed to draw the man's attention as he staggered away from me and towards Jen. I began to think that this could work to my advantage in giving me some time to get Sam out of the car.

Soon enough, Jen reached the hardware store. With the man several steps behind her, she fumbled with the keys and quickly got the door open and ran inside.

I sighed with relief and began focusing my attention on getting Sam out of the car safely. I reached through the shattered window and grabbed her by the arm, once again saying her name. She didn't respond, but when I gently shook her, I heard her moan slightly—giving me a little more hope.

I quickly looked back at the store to see the man slapping his blood-covered hands on the glass door. Jen was on the other side, anxiously waiting for me to pull Sam free. I took a breath and dragged Sam up towards me. She was pretty light and surprisingly easy to lift out of the car.

I got her out of the car and held her unconscious body in my arms. As I was about to head to the store, I realized the infected man was still at the entrance. Immediately, I thought of him following Fido's bark and I shouted at the top of my lungs, "Hey!"

The man looked over at me with a lifeless look in his eyes—his mouth agape, his eyes strange and lifeless, dry blood covering much of his pale skin. Sure enough, he began stumbling in my direction.

I was pretty confident that these things were incapable of reasoning, so I shouted, "Unlock the door Jen!" The man was fixated on me and slowly began its pursuit. As he stumbled back across the road, I tried my best to egg him on, "Come here! Come on, asshole!" Although, it probably didn't matter what I said, so long as I made noise.

As he got about ten feet from us, I began to move as quickly as I could around him—moving towards the store, yet keeping my distance from him.

"Come on, Pete!" Jen shouted from the door.

I looked over to see the door open and Jen waiting for me to get inside with Sam. I tried to move faster while still holding her in my arms.

The man reached his arms out at me as I ran a semi-circle around him and made my way to the door. Jen guided us in and quickly locked the door behind us.

Fido continued barking as he watched the infected man walk back to the door, and began banging on it again. I laid Sam down on the floor and let out a sigh of relief. For now at least, we were safe.

TARA

As I sat in the middle of the walk-in fridge, I began wondering if this was really happening. So many things ran through my head. I wondered if the cops would come or if an ambulance was on its way. I wanted to tell my boyfriend what was happening, to see if he knew anything more than me.

Suddenly, I realized my cell phone was in my apron pocket, something I didn't normally carry with me at work. I immediately took it out and saw a large 'X' where the service bars should've been. It made sense; not many phones are likely to get service inside the thick insulated walls of a double-XL refrigerator.

I began pacing through the small, cold room full of cheese, frozen pizza dough, and metal shelving, holding my phone as if it were a compass.

Only the 'north' I was looking for was any kind of cellular service. Finally, when I got close enough to the vent, one tiny bar of service popped up in the top corner of the screen. I flipped open my phone and tried to call him. As the call attempted to go through, my phone began to ring in my ear. Startled, I almost dropped it, and then I looked at the screen and saw it was my boyfriend!

Immediately, I answered it and nearly screamed his name with joy. However, I was greeted with nothing more than a broken-apart voice trying to say, "Hello?" I had slightly moved during all the excitement and lost the signal. So, I sat atop one of the shelves and nearly stuck my head into the vent, where the walls were the least thick, and once again attempted the call.

Finally, I got hold of him. He was calling to see if I was okay and told me that something bad had happened and was all over the news. But he wasn't able to tell me exactly what was going on as every station seemed to be broadcasting the events alongside theories—mostly wacky theories. He did tell me about the commonality of biting during all of this, which confirmed that the same thing had happened here.

Soon enough, I explained my current situation to him, and he said he was already on his way to rescue me. He attempted to call the police, but the lines were busy—this really was a slap of reality, showing how serious this situation had become. I was nervous.

I lost service a few more times, as it was hard to keep my phone in the right place. Eventually, I lost service and was off the phone for a few long minutes. I broke down; I didn't know what to think. I cried. It was quiet.

I could hear someone moving around on the other side of the fridge door. I pressed my head up against the cold door and listened. It sounded like someone was moving past it, possibly dragging something on the floor. I listened intently, wondering what was happening, trying to picture the state of things now — where I once worked and mingled with friends — now riddled with blood and bodies.

Suddenly, my phone, which was sitting by the vent, rang again. I ran to it and answered. It was my boyfriend. "I'm by the movie theater," he said. "There's a bunch of people up ahead. I don't know what's going on."

"Do you think it's safe?" I asked.

"Well, there's so many of them, maybe they're trying to get something organized. I'm gonna try to get through."

I sat and listened to what was happening. I heard him yell to someone, "Hey! Sir? Excuse me?" I waited anxiously to hear a normal and healthy voice respond. But it was to no avail as I only heard someone shouting, followed by my boyfriend's voice coming back on the phone. "Something's wrong with them!"

"Get out of there!" I screamed.

He sounded panicked and I heard the screeching of his tires quickly pulling away. I heard something — a bang or a crash — then, nothing for a moment until I heard heavy breathing coming from someone. I sat and listened, trying to figure out what to do. I heard him again. "Oh shit!"

At this point, I began shouting his name, but his voice sounded far away, as if he were holding his phone or had it in his pocket. Next, I think I heard his car door swing open followed by quick footsteps. It sounded like a quick gust of wind and the call ended. I stared at my phone for a moment, wondering if I should call back. I tried and it went straight to voicemail. I had no idea what just happened. I sat there, not sure of what to do next.

I got up and looked around. I couldn't sit around forever in a locked walk-in refrigerator waiting for someone to find me.

I took a large bread roller in my hands and slowly went to the door to open it.

MIKE

Kelly and I walked through an empty town, keeping distance from anything or anyone we saw moving off in the distance as we attempted to digest the information we were just fed over the radio. Eventually, we came across a seemingly untouched building with the lights still on. If you blocked out everything else, you could've looked at this establishment and thought that everything was normal in suburbia.

We slowly approached and went inside the '24-Hour Laundromat.' At first, it didn't look as if there was anything of use or interest, as the place didn't even have a bathroom or vending machine—never mind a phone. But just as I began to write the place off as a waste of time, Kelly spotted a door in the back with a sign: **Keep Out – Office Space**.

We approached the door and heard absolutely nothing coming from the other side, and decided it was worth a look. Of course, the door was locked. Kelly pushed her small frame against it a few times. It wasn't a huge door, but it wasn't budging either. I had to help—regardless of my previously dislocated shoulder. We took down the door with a synchronized three-count. Thankfully, we found a small room with a desk, piles of paperwork—more than one would expect a laundromat to produce, and an old rotary phone.

I took the plunge and made a call to my house. It went through and rang for a minute until it went to voicemail. After the 'beep,' I sat there silently, just waiting and thinking. Kelly was off in the corner, trying to make it look like she was doing something, but I'm certain she was just trying to give me space. After a moment, I hung up the phone and she slightly glanced up at me. I shook my head and for the first time began to break down a little.

She came over and put her hand on my back. At this point, I dropped the picture I'd taken from my car, of my daughter. She picked it up and stared at the photo for a moment before turning it over and reading, *"Ellie–Christmas 2009."*

She handed me the picture as I struggled to say, "It's my…my daughter."

"Just because there wasn't an answer doesn't mean anything," Kelly explained. "I mean, we're not at *our* homes and we're okay—well, sort of okay."

I smiled at her and nodded.

"You heard all of the safe zones they mentioned on the radio?" Kelly asked. "They're probably at one of those."

She was probably right; at least I wanted to believe she was. Kelly was an awesome person from what I could tell. We were stuck in an extraordinary situation together as strangers and it seemed I'd developed a better relationship with her than with any other female since my ex-wife, Ellie's mother. Of course, who knows if Kelly was feeling the same way. For all I knew, she had a boyfriend—or a girlfriend. In another time or place, perhaps we would have talked about it.

The 'moment' was cut short when we heard noises coming from outside the office. Kelly quickly peeked outside the door and saw a couple of infected stumbling about. Then I realized the word 'infected' wasn't the most correct word to use. 'Undead' would work just as well. I decided it didn't really matter and either description was apt.

I held the broken door closed as we discussed a plan of how to handle the infected/undead people.

As we spoke quietly to one another, an infected man over by the washing machines must have heard us, came over to us, and soon enough began slapping his lifeless hands against the door. Kelly and I looked at one another and knew we'd run out of options. We either had to get the hell out of Dodge or we were going to become lunch for this ghoul.

We decided to act.

I remained at the door as Kelly got the shotgun ready. She nodded and I grabbed the doorknob and slowly pulled the door open. The undead man stumbled into the small office, almost falling to the floor. Quickly, Kelly took the shot, and as the shotgun recoiled, the blast broke straight through the seemingly fragile skull and destroyed whatever brain the man had, sending the undead thing back to the dead.

"Good shot," I said to Kelly, trying not to think about the fact that a dead man lay right between us with half his head missing. She nodded, and without saying a word, looked out of the office where two more undead people were stumbling towards us. They were moving slowly between the benches and washing machines, and we had a relatively clear path to the exit.

"We need to move," she said and held up the shotgun. "I don't want to use this if I don't have to, or I'll run out of shells."

I nodded and began to step to the door. She grabbed a broom leaning against the wall and handed it to me. "Keep them back with this," she said.

We evacuated the building as quickly as possible. Kelly used her shotgun to push one of them back. It fell over a bench and landed hard on the floor, but was unfazed by the bump it had taken. The thing got back up slowly and continued its pursuit of us. By this time, though, we'd escaped the laundromat and were running down the street, looking back at the handful of infected that were being drawn in our direction after all of the commotion.

As we ran, we passed confused-looking people who had been infected, stumbling by themselves aimlessly, and worst of all, feeding frenzies with nearly a dozen at a time huddled together eating someone. These primitive creatures barely noticed us as we ran by stealthily. And, if they did notice us, we outran them until they lost interest. We decided to be as quick and quiet as possible until we came to a good place to rest.

We ran through many streets as my legs cramped up as bad as some of my worst bike races, but I didn't allow myself to stop. Finally, Kelly began to slow down in front of me—several yards in front, as I simply couldn't keep up with her.

"Look, it's a school," she said. "Should be a good place to take a break."

It was brilliant thinking. A school during the summertime was bound to be empty. We quickly walked around the perimeter of what looked to be a junior high school, seeing no signs of the living—or the dead. We stopped at the back of the school near a loading dock and took a rest. It was a fenced-in area on three sides so we figured, short of being inside the building, it was the safest place we could be from any wandering infected.

Kelly sat down on the loading dock and put down the shotgun. I attempted to stretch out my cramping legs as well as tend to my shoulder, which still felt quite tender after the bicycle crash from earlier.

We discussed the possibility of hiding inside the school but were unsure of our method of entry considering the only doors nearby were locked. As I brought up the idea of once again taking another walk around the school to survey the different entrances, we began to hear a shuffling noise coming from somewhere close by.

Kelly and I looked around, our eyes darting left and right. There were lights on around the building, so it wasn't too dark. We couldn't see anything coming from any direction and I began to wonder if it was simply an animal somewhere.

Kelly looked at me and smirked. "I think we're okay."

As she began to let her guard down, there came a scratching noise followed by a bloody arm reaching through the side opening of a dumpster a few feet from Kelly. The man was fast, faster than I would have expected. He lunged from his hiding place and grabbed Kelly's arm. She screamed as the man pulled her towards the dumpster.

The tearing of flesh and cloth came from behind the dumpster as the infected school janitor attacked Kelly, his teeth tearing into her arm. She quickly reached for her shotgun and in the struggle, knocked it off the loading dock and to the ground.

At this point, I ran to the shotgun and grasped it in my hand. As I picked it up, I witnessed what was left of the janitor curl his dried lips up and over his blood-stained teeth, and in one fell swoop, bit through the flesh of Kelly's neck. She screamed in horror as I yelled in fear. The janitor looked at me with Kelly's blood dripping from his mouth. With no hesitation, I pulled the trigger and sent his lifeless carcass back into the trash heap.

While holding her torn neck, Kelly fell to the ground. Blood poured through her fingers. I dropped the shotgun and rushed to Kelly's side. She looked at me as tears streamed down her face.

"Get out of here, Mike," she said to me through bloody bubbles. A large blood pool was beneath her, and I knew she was bleeding out fast.

I shook my head and tried to pick her up, but she gently squeezed my hand and looked at me for a moment before letting it go. Then her eyes closed and her body seemed to go limp as she let out one last breath.

I knew what would happen if I stayed and I didn't have the heart to shoot her when she revived as one of them.

I backed away, turned, and once again began running with the shotgun in my hand. I ran for what seemed like miles without thinking until finally I saw a small building with the lights on. I had no idea if it was safe or not, but my legs just stopped and I dropped to my knees, staring at the lighted building ahead.

JEN

Sam seemed okay other than some bumps and bruises. She hasn't said anything at all in relation to Robbie since arriving at the hardware store. Pete took her into the back and made a makeshift bed for her out of a fire blanket.

The infected man that had been outside and banging on the door finally wandered away and for the moment the street was empty.

In the meantime, I decided to stay by the front windows to see if anyone came by that could help us. I was hoping for a police car, ambulance, or a fire truck, anything to help the situation. No one came. That is until I saw a different man stumble into the parking lot and then into the street. He had some blood on him but he moved in such a way that I could see he wasn't one of them. He was carrying a gun, too - a shotgun by the looks of it.

"Pete!" I yelled. "Come quick!"

Of course, in a situation like this, he came running as fast as he could. Realizing he probably thought I was hurt, I quickly added, "There's a man outside and he looks okay!"

Pete joined me at the window and looked out at the disheveled man. Fido began barking from the manager's office where Peter had placed him when we'd arrived, in an effort to keep him quiet.

Ignoring the barking, we both approached the front door and Peter quickly unlocked it.

"Hello? Do you need help?" I called to the man in the street.

He looked up and I think I saw him smile a little. "We have to help him," I said to Peter as I tried to go outside.

Peter held me back and shouted, "Are you sick?"

The man looked up and shook his head no and gave us a *thumbs up*. At this point, Peter and I ran out to him. Peter took the shotgun out of the man's hand, and we helped him into the hardware store.

He sat down and we got him some water. He drank deeply.

"Thank you," he said after taking a breathe.

"What's your name?" Peter asked.

He closed his eyes for a moment as if he had to think about it. "Mike, my name's Mike."

"Are you okay?" I asked.

He nodded slowly in response and seemed to struggle to keep his eyes open. At this point, Peter and I helped him to the back where Samantha had fallen asleep.

"Here, Mike," Peter said. "Rest now. We'll talk more, later."

"Thank you," Mike said. "Who are you guys?"

"Oh, I'm Peter."

"I'm Jen."

He smiled at us as he lay down on floor, using some cardboard for bedding. Peter and I returned to the front window and continued our vigil.

TARA

I fought my way out of the walk-in fridge and past several sick-looking customers until I came across Teddy in the kitchen who was now covered in blood and growling and reaching for me. As he came around the counter, he lunged violently in my direction.

I pushed him back with the bread roller and proceeded to hit him hard in the jaw with it. It looked as if his jaw broke in two as he fell hard into the metal counter top once covered in pizza sauce and now covered in blood. I ran for the exit and tossed the bloody bread roller on the ground.

As I left my workplace—possibly for the last time ever, I ran through the parking lot repeating to myself, "The movie theater, the movie theater..." I was going to find out what happened to my boyfriend before anything else.

As I approached my car, I realized, I did not have my keys with me. I didn't have anything except my work uniform and my cell phone. I looked back at the restaurant and saw Teddy coming out the door after me. I took off running at this point.

I quickly ran a couple blocks, past such surreal scenes that I could barely comprehend if they were real or not. For the most part, the streets were abandoned with crashed and idle cars strewn about.

Eventually, I came across his car, sitting with the driver's door ajar in the middle of the road. As I approached the car, I found his cell phone laying in two pieces on the ground. I continued walking to the car and saw no signs of blood around—which gave me some hope, but not much.

As I got to the car, I heard the soft beeping sound that cars make when the keys are left in the ignition while the door is open. I hopped in and turned the key. The engine took a second to roll over as I noticed the gas light had come on.

I began to drive in the direction it looked like he had gone. There was no sign of anyone anywhere. I continued to drive, looking for anyone that could be of assistance.

I didn't make it far before the engine began to sputter as the gas tank was on empty. I coasted the car into a hardware store parking lot where I was shocked to see two people watching me from the front window of the store.

PETER

As the sun started to rise, I was the only one awake. Jen was asleep with Sam in the stockroom. And, the new arrivals Tara and Mike were each sound asleep as well. Both were each shaken up pretty bad upon their arrivals. It made me think of how strangely lucky Sam, Jen and I are. At least we were here together though all this. Tara and Mike were alone.

The infected have been roaming the streets all night. I turned off the main lights in the store shortly after Tara showed up, been running on flashlights ever since. The streetlights are pretty good on this street though, so it has been easy for me to see them—yet hard for them to see me.

Before Jen went to get some sleep, we got Mike's gun and anything else we could use as a weapon together—blunt objects—

mostly shovels. We thought it would be best to keep these things near the entrance if needed.

Also, Fido has been sleeping on the ground next to me. He finally started to calm down a few hours ago so I took him out of the office and was able to get him some water. He went to the bathroom a few times in the office and seemed quite stressed out, I'm glad to see him get some rest. For some reason, watching Fido drink the water and act like a normal dog in a normal situation reminded me of my mom, so I decided to hop on the store phone and give her a call.

I had a contact number for her while she was on vacation in Toronto visiting her sister. So, I called her and got no answer. It went to my aunt's voicemail. I didn't leave a message. I had to believe things weren't like this in Canada. Although, she had to know what has been happening here. I know it's selfish but I hope she's worried about me. Better that than the alternative. I hope she's okay.

Speaking of animals, I've been watching birds fly around outside, coming and going as they please. The thing is, they flew relatively close to some infected people and drew no reaction—this makes me think that these things are only after people, not just any form of meat, or dare I say, sustenance.

Once everyone wakes up, Jen and I were thinking of playing around with the bunny ear antennae on the old TV in the office to see if we could find out some news about what's going on.

As it got lighter outside, I began to worry about them seeing me inside the store. Soon enough, my fears were confirmed as a man wearing a crimson coated shirt and sporting only one arm began stumbling across the parking lot. A few others stumbled through the parking lot during the night, but this one seemed to be coming straight towards the window.

Quickly, I looked up and down the street to see no other infected persons in either direction. So, I grabbed one of the shovels and decided to get rid of the threat.

JEN

After sleeping for a few hours, I came out to the sales floor to meet Peter by the window and see if we could get the TV working. Fido came to greet me, but I was shocked and surprised when I looked outside to see Peter facing off with a sick man.

Scared, I quickly approached the window. "Peter!" I shouted. The infected man looked up at me with his bloody and blank eyes. Knowing there was a window between us helped a little, but I can't explain the death stare I felt coming from him. As the man stared at me, Peter swung the shovel like a baseball bat at the back of its skull. Blood splattered on the shovel as the man fell hard to the ground. Peter looked up at me with anger written on his face as I motioned for him to come back inside.

Peter ran inside and I greeted him with a hug. After we locked the door behind him, Peter placed his shovel down, and removed his bloody shirt, replacing it with a *Fix-It Hardware* t-shirt.

"What were you thinking?" I asked.

He simply replied, "I had to…"

I continued to hug him for a moment as he stood there emotionless. Then, Mike came through the swinging stockroom doors. He looked around the hardware store for a moment and then at us.

"Hi, guys," Mike said in a pretty monotonous tone.

"Morning," I said.

"Hi, Mike," Peter said. "How are you doing?"

Mike shook his head. "I guess this wasn't just a dream…"

"Yeah, I know," Pete replied. "We're going to check out the news and see what's happening."

Mike nodded, "Sounds good. Is there a phone I can use first?"

Pete pointed to the cashier's station. "Go for it."

"Thank you."

It was hard to read how Mike was feeling. He hadn't said much about the night before so we had no idea what he had been through. He came to us, holding a shotgun with only two bullets—or shells I guess, and he was covered in little scrapes and bruises. Needless to say, he looked like a mess. Also, he had been holding his shoulder almost nonstop. Pete asked him last night if it was okay and Mike said, "Just a little sore, it was a rough night." It wasn't bleeding or anything and other than the little cuts he had, it didn't look like he had any wounds or, more specifically, any bites.

That being said, Tara was just about as mysterious. She pulled into the parking lot with a car with no gas left. We weren't even sure if the car was hers or if she found or stole it. She didn't seem like the criminal type, but then again, I don't think one would have to be to steal a car in a situation like this.

She wasn't nearly as banged up as Mike, but she was sporting a waitress uniform that was covered in dry blood. I couldn't even imagine how her work shift went... It was very evident that whatever she had been through was quite traumatic as she lightly cried herself to sleep once we got her situated in the stock room.

Peter and I seemed to be unofficially in charge of the small group that had formed overnight. Sam seems to be very distant after what had happened to Robbie and I don't think she's going to get much better anytime soon.

I just hope that we can hold things together until help arrives. We're going to start fiddling around with the TV soon. Once Mike finishes his phone call, we'll start figuring it out while one of us stays by the window. This will probably have to be Peter or myself as I'm not sure if we can trust Mike to keep watch by himself—he still seems pretty fragile or vulnerable at this time.

MIKE

Using the store's phone, I once again tried to get in touch with my ex to see if she and Ellie were okay. Unfortunately, I had the same luck as when I tried in the Laundromat—no answer. Perhaps I would try again soon, but I was pretty sure they had left… Hopefully, they've made it somewhere safe and secure; away from all of this.

I stood at the phone for a moment, looking around this hardware shop. I kept thinking how normal everything looked. Various products were displayed everywhere, sale signs promoting **Summer Specials**. I tried to imagine that I was just there to buy some tools for yard work or something along those lines. However, my attempt to escape from reality was short-lived as I glanced out the front window to see a car flipped on its side across the street—I was told this was the car Peter, Jen and Samantha used to get here… They must've had quite an experience.

As troubled as I was that I was unable to reach my daughter, I was very intrigued by Peter's idea of trying to get some news on the TV in the manager's office. Perhaps we could figure out what exactly was happening and how long we're going to have to wait this out.

As I stood there with my mind traveling through various thoughts, Peter walked up to me and handed me a mug that said **Fix-It** on the side with a little cartoon hammer next to it.

"What is this?" I asked.

"The manager was—uh, is—he has a ton of instant coffee in his office," Peter said to me.

"That's great news," I said. "Thanks!"

Peter nodded as he handed me the lukewarm cup of coffee, likely made from hot water from the tap. But, it was still good for what it was... It was strangely comforting.

As I sipped my cup, Peter glanced at the phone and looked at me. I knew what he was going to ask so I simply said, "I didn't get through."

"Sorry," he said.

I tried not to think about it. "What about this TV situation?" I asked.

"Jen's been playing with the antennae."

"Should we go see how she's doing?" I asked.

Before Peter could answer, his little dog came running to us.

"Fido," Peter said.

I smirked as I looked at the curious pup sniffing around my shoes.

"Hey, guys," Jen said from the other room. "I think I've almost got it!"

"Nice!" Peter said, enthusiastically.

As we were about to go check out the TV, the stock room doors slowly opened and one of the other girls, Tara, came through them.

"Hi," she said.

Peter and I smiled at her. Jen came out of the office.

"Hey, Tara," she said. "How'd you sleep?"

Tara shrugged. "Okay, thanks."

"We're trying to get the news to come in on the TV," Peter explained to her.

"Oh," she said, "the other girl back there is awake, but she wouldn't say anything to me."

Jen and Peter looked at each other; you could see the concern written all over their faces.

"Let me go back there," Jen said.

"Yeah, go," Peter said. "Tara and Mike can help me check out the TV."

PETER

Jen went to check on Sam while the rest of us took a look at the TV. We were all very anxious to hear what was happening outside. I kept thinking they had to have contained it by now with all the advancements in medicine. This thought eased my anxiety but was quickly overridden with the but what if they haven't thought.

I got Tara a cup of instant coffee and we all headed into the office. Fido followed us and was very curious about Tara and Mike. Tara seemed to like Fido a lot and was picking him up and petting him most of the time while Mike and I attempted to get a picture on the old TV.

The picture came and went as we started to hear jumbled sounds. An anchor that I had never seen before was talking as names of locations scrolled across the bottom of the screen.

"The events have contin…" the anchorman said but static interfered with the audio.

I looked at Mike and Tara as they stared at the screen, waiting and hoping for the connection to settle and news to come through.

"Come on. Work, please," I said.

Mike sat forward and gently smacked the side of the TV. The picture jumbled for a moment, mixing up the different colors. Then, as if it was a snow globe, the picture came together as the colors and hues settled into their correct positions and the static-filled audio warped a little until the seemingly amateur anchor's voice settled into a steady tone.

"Good job, Mike!"

"Thanks," he said to me.

Suddenly, Jen showed up in the doorway. "It works?" she asked, excitedly.

"How's Sam?" I asked.

Then, Sam peaked around the corner with a blank look on her face.

"How are you feeling?" I asked her.

She simply shrugged her shoulders and walked away.

"I'm going to sit by the window with her for a while," Jen said. "You guys check out the news and let me know what they say."

I nodded as Jen followed Sam to the front of the store.

THE TELEVISON

ANDREW HELMS: "This is Andrew Helms, reporting live for the 'Channel Five Emergency News.' The time is now 12:14 p.m. on June 14th. It has now been over twenty-four hours since the first infection became apparent. What was once believed to be riots followed by severe acts of violence is now known as an epidemic which has been labeled the 'Arthriphagy Virus' by Doctor Joanne Sanders at Massachusetts General Hospital. Doctor Sanders was one of the first Doctors in the New England area to inspect the rapid-spreading disease. We will now go to a previously recorded interview with Doctor Sanders."

CUT TO: MASS GENERAL HOSPITAL (TITLE: PREVIOUSLY RECORDED: JUNE 13 APPROXIMATELY 11:30 A.M.)

JOANNE SANDERS: "This disease is one I have never encountered in my 25 years of practicing medicine. After treating several patients, we are led to believe the virus begins with a bite wound. Depending on the severity of the bite, symptoms may take effect within one hour, though we have taken in two bite victims whom have not shown symptoms, yet have been bit for over two hours."

INTERVIEWER: "What exactly are these symptoms, Doctor?"

JOANNE SANDERS: "Well, the symptoms seem to vary between individuals. Thus far, each patient I have examined has shown slight discoloration, a fever, usually around 103 degrees Fahrenheit, and dizziness. However, some patients have exhibited profuse vomiting, slight loss of memory, and severe numbness, mostly of the lower body."

INTERVIEWER: "And, how many Arthriphagy patients have been treated so far?"

JOANNE SANDERS: "I personally examined about twelve patients this morning. Other staff members have also examined patients. But, as to how many have been treated... I regret to say, none have been treated successfully. At this time no cure for the Arthriphagy virus is known."

INTERVIEWER: "Are we to understand all of the patients examined have become fully infected by the virus?"

JOANNE SANDERS: "That is correct, other than the two I mentioned previously, all patients have exhibited full infection after a period of time. Once the infection takes full effect, there is no readable pulse, and the person's body temperature rapidly drops, to the point of being unidentifiable by our thermometers. The patients become 100% non-communicable as well."

INTERVIEWER: "With no pulse, are we to consider these infected people alive or dead?"

JOANNE SANDERS: "I... I'm sorry. I can't answer any more questions."

CUT TO: NEWS STUDIO

ANDREW HELMS: "For those of you just tuning in, that was a previously recorded interview with Doctor Sanders of Massachusetts General Hospital. It was recorded approximately twenty-four hours ago. Still, no cure for the Arthriphagy Virus has been found. Mass General has locked off a quarantine area for those infected with the virus. And, as of fifteen hours ago, the staff at Mass General has temporarily locked their doors, not allowing anyone seeking medical assistance into the facility. However, if you are out there, and seeking medical assistance, military bases have been stationed throughout the New England area, as well as New York City and upstate New York. However, rather than seeking these bases yourselves, government officials are urging everyone to stay indoors, locking all doors and windows. Rescue squads have been released and will be looking for any and all survivors. On that note, I would like to go live via satellite to Officer David Stephens in Danvers, Massachusetts."

CUT TO: MILITARY REFUGE BASE, DANVERS, MA.

ANDREW HELMS: "Officer, thank you for joining us."

DAVID STEPHENS: "Hello, thank you."

ANDREW HELMS: "Officer, can you tell us what the current plan is for the base in Danvers?"

DAVID STEPHENS: "Well, right now, we are securing several buildings in the area. The National Guard, police service, and surrounding towns' fire departments are here to help and things seem to be coming together. At this time we have dispatched eight search and rescue helicopters throughout central and eastern Massachusetts, as well as several ground units. If you're out there, stay put, stay safe, and if possible set off some flares or make some signs to help us locate you. But, if you're out there, we will find you and relocate you to our current safe zone."

ANDREW HELMS: "What exactly do you mean by 'current' safe zone?"

DAVID STEPHENS: "Should we have to relocate our base. Springfield had a large safe zone, but they began to become over-run with the infected, therefore what was left of the base had to relocate to Warren, Massachusetts. They too have many search and rescue teams searching central and western Massachusetts."

ANDREW HELMS: "And, has your team had to deal with Arthriphagy carriers since setting up your safe zone?"

DAVID STEPHENS: "Yes, we have. Currently, we have teams going through the building behind me, and one other building, clearing them of any infected people."

ANDREW HELMS: "And, may I ask, by what means are you 'clearing out the infected'?"

DAVID STEPHENS: "Unfortunately, we have resorted to putting down the infected by using deadly force—one bullet to the head. So far, there is no other known method of killing the infected other than severe trauma to the head and or brain. We do have a small containment zone of a dozen infected—"

(A static coating forms over the satellite feed.)

ANDREW HELMS: "Officer? Officer Stephens?"

CUT TO: NEWS STUDIO

ANDREW HELMS: "Hello? Officer Stephens? It appears that we have lost our satellite feed to Officer David Stephens. Nonetheless, search and rescue teams are all over the state of Massachusetts, so stay where you are, and they will find you."

FADE TO BLACK.

CUT TO: NEWS STUDIO

ANDREW HELMS: "Welcome back to 'Channel five Emergency News.' This is Andrew Helms. The time is now 11:47 p.m., on June 14th. The recent epidemic of the Arthriphagy virus—or A. Phagy as it is now being referred to as, has now spread throughout the Great Lakes region of the United States. All we can tell you now is the whole country is under a state of emergency. At Midnight, we will be going live via satellite to the White House where we will hear directly from the President himself. And, as an update, we've been told search and rescue teams are still traveling via helicopter only. I repeat: no official ground units are traveling as search and rescue. Hope is not lost for those out there. Many helicopters will be traveling all over the state of Massachusetts. Signs on roofs and flares are still highly recommended for those still looking for rescue...

"This just in, Massachusetts General Hospital has been evacuated. All staff and patients unrelated to the Arthriphagy virus have been moved to a safe zone in Warren, Massachusetts. The safe zone in Danvers was evacuated not long ago, and the National Guard, military personnel, police and fire rescue, and volunteers have moved across the state borders into a safe zone in Hampton, New Hampshire.

"I'm being told we are going live via satellite right now to the White House, to hear from the Secretary of Defense."

CUT TO: WHITE HOUSE CONFERENCE ROOM
(Many people are raising hands and shouting questions in a chaotic fashion.)
SECRETARY OF DEFENSE: "Please! Please! Quiet! The President will be available shortly. However, I have some information and will be able to answer any questions you may have. It is evident that the Arthriphagy virus has spread throughout most of the Eastern states. Health inspectors are speculating the possibility

of it being an airborne virus. Also, many believe it could be an act of terrorism. We would like to say that this is not likely."

(A few people in the crowd raise their voices.)

"Please! The other possibility is a biochemical infection resulting from a spill or accident of some kind. We have officials throughout New York and New England searching for evidence to support this theory, however, nothing has become evident as of yet."

(A couple people shout out some questions again.)

"I'll be able to answer your questions in a moment. Let me tell you what we know to be fact. This virus is highly contagious; the main transport for the disease is via a bite. Though this is definitely one way the disease can be caught, it is not known if it can spread in other fashions. We do not recommend any direct contact with the infected.

I will now take your questions."

REPORTER 1: "The virus has spread to the Great Lakes, what, if any, plans of containment do you have?"

SECRETARY OF DEFENSE: "Safe zones are being established in each state across the country, as well as in Canada and Northern Mexico. We have no doubt that within the next forty-eight to seventy-two hours we will have everything under control. Next question please."

REPORTER 2: "Are those infected with the virus considered alive or dead?"

SECRETARY OF DEFENSE: "Next question!"

(The people go crazy, asking questions non-stop.)

"No more questions!"

CUT TO: NEWS STUDIO
ANDREW HELMS: "This just in. We will be going live to Doctor Charles Porter at the National office of the Entomological Society of America in Lanham, Maryland."
CUT TO: ENTOMOLOGICAL SOCIETY OF AMERICA
ANDREW HELMS: "Doctor, thank you for joining us."
DR.CHARLES PORTER: "Not at all."
ANDREW HELMS: "Evidence has shown us that the Arthriphagy virus is primarily spread through bite wounds. What we would like to know is: would it be possible for this rapidly spreading disease to be transported through the bite of insects such as mosquitoes or ticks?"
DR. CHARLES PORTER: "It is uncertain at this time. But, diseases such as Malaria, Lyme and the all too familiar West Nile can be, while Human Immunodeficiency Virus and Human Papilloma Virus cannot. This Arthriphagy virus is extremely complex with how quickly it can spread. Therefore, it is only a matter of time until we can be sure if insects such as mosquitoes could be a possible mode of transport."
ANDREW HELMS: "So, do *you* think it's possible that the Arthriphagy virus could be spread through mosquitoes?"
DR. CHARLES PORTER: "It certainly is possible. However, the rapid decay rate evident in human hosts infected with the virus does bring forth the idea that the virus would simply kill mosquitoes, or even ticks."

CUT TO: NEWS STUDIO
ANDREW HELMS: "That was Dr. Charles Porter from the Entomological Society of America, offering us a somewhat different, yet relevant view on the Arthriphagy epidemic.

"The time is now 11:55 p.m., on June 14th. We are still expecting to hear live via satellite from the President of the United States at midnight.

"As an update, the A. Phagy virus continues to spread throughout the United States. Good news however, over ten rescues in the state of Massachusetts have been reported in the past hour. Again, search and rescue teams are out via helicopter only right now. We strongly urge those out there, seeking rescue, to stay somewhere indoors, somewhere secure. If you're just tuning in, we suggest making some sort of a sign on your roof, allowing search and rescue units to locate you easier. We also highly recommend the use of flares, especially now, when it is dark out.

"Safe zones are now being established throughout the United States, including those states currently free of infection. Current safe zones established in the New England area are officially being patrolled by the National Guard. For an updated listing of these safe zones, please tune in to the AM radio stations listed below."

(A list of locations and AM radio stations appears on the bottom of the screen.)

"Updates will be made to this list as necessary. And this list will be shown throughout the remainder of this broadcast. However long that may be.

"This just in, a search and rescue helicopter in Lakeville, Massachusetts, has been taken down. At what first appeared to be a mob of people seeking rescue, turned out to be a group of hosts infected with the virus. All search and rescue units in New England have returned to their respective safe zones and have suspended any search and rescue missions until daylight.

"We urge the people still out there to stay put, and if you are using flares or any other limited resource to seek rescue, please stop until daylight. Ration these resources and as long as I am on the air, I will do my best to tell you the best time to use them.

"The time is now 12:01 a.m. on June 15th. We understand the President of the United States will be available shortly with any and all current information that may be available. And we apologize for the delay.

"As we return to the rescue helicopter story, we're now being told that the helicopter was landing in the backyard of a residence in Lakeville. We do not know the exact number of casualties at this time. Though we can tell you, the helicopter took off with three rescuers from the safe zone in Warren, Massachusetts. Whether or not these three people were volunteers or National Guard soldiers, we cannot be sure at this time.

"For those of you just tuning in please do not use any limited resources such as flares until otherwise directed to as all search and rescue units have been suspended until daylight. I repeat - all search and rescue units have been suspended until daylight. An updated list of locations and AM radio stations are scrolling along the bottom of the screen. I'm being told that we have received a previously-recorded video from the safe zone in Warren, Massachusetts. This should be available shortly.

"Also, we still plan to go live via satellite to the President of the United States. We apologize again for the delay. I'm being told we are now switching over to a video previously recorded at about 1:00 p.m. yesterday."

CUT TO: MILITARY SAFEZONE
(Three soldiers stand in front of a large fenced-in area of a dozen infected people stumbling around aimlessly, and a few against the fence, reaching for the soldiers.)
DENNIS HARDY: "Hello, America, I'm Sergeant Dennis Hardy. Here we've got about a dozen of these infected... We're

here to show you some safety precautions you should take if you should encounter an infected person."

(One of the three soldiers slowly unlocks the gate to the fenced-in area.)

"What we're going to do is let one of the infected out to show you just how to take care of them in a one-on-one situation."

(The soldier removes the lock and chain, and simply holds the gate shut while the other two soldiers hold long poles in the area, keeping the infected people back."

SOLDIER: "Ready, Sergeant!"

DENNIS HARDY: "Okay, in this situation I am going to use a pistol to demonstrate how to take down the infected host."

"Okay! Let one out!"

(The soldiers carefully let one out and hold a few back. One infected person steps out of the area and is pushed with the poles towards Dennis, who quickly holds up his pistol towards the infected, now stumbling towards him)

"Okay, here we go!"

(Dennis backs up quickly and doesn't fire his gun.)

"You gotta stay on your feet. Don't let 'em get too close to you. Okay, what I'm about to do is show y'all what is not affective in killing these things."

(Dennis stops and shoots his pistol once. He shoots the infected in the left arm, towards the shoulder. The infected stumbles backward for a moment before regaining its balance.)

"As you can see, this is hardly affective."

(He shoots the infected person in the right knee. It falls but doesn't appear to be in pain.)

"See? Naturally, this will knock him down. But, if you're looking to kill this thing permanently, this ain't the way to go. Now, I will show you the only way to permanently kill one of these things."

(As the infected person struggles to stand up, Hardy walks over to it and shoots it point blank in the head. The back of its head opens and dark crimson blood bursts out and sprays the ground and fence behind as the infected person falls back to the ground and remains motionless.)

"You see, the only way to kill one of these things, is a bullet in the brain. In a situation where you cannot get a head-shot, the most effective thing to do would be to go for the knees. It makes it almost impossible for one of 'em to get up. Now, we understand not everyone out there owns a firearm. So, we will now show you some options, using more household objects—"

CUT TO: NEWS STUDIO

ANDREW HELMS: "We're sorry for the interruption. But, we will be going live via satellite, to the President of the United States right now."

CUT TO: OVAL OFFICE

PRESIDENT: "My fellow Americans. June 13th is a day that will live in infamy. The United States of America has seemingly become overrun with a virus that has been labeled the Arthriphagy virus. This is containable and, without a doubt, curable. I ask those out there to seek refuge somewhere safe and secure, especially those on the west coast. Where there is little sign of infection, for safety sake, please relocate yourselves to your local safe zone. Those on the east coast, outside of a safe zone, please stay where you are. Signs on the rooftops are helpful to our search teams and listen for helicopters. We have teams all over the country, as well as the best doctors in the world developing a cure as we speak. In no less than 72 hours we will have this situation entirely under control. Remain at your current location until our search and rescue units locate you. This is an obstacle like no other. But, we will overcome. America will overcome. Mankind will overcome. May God be with us through these trying days."

CUT TO: NEWS STUDIO
ANDREW HELMS: "That was the President of the United States live via satellite. The time is now 12:20 a.m. on June 15th. Nearly two days since the outbreak of the Arthriphagy virus. We will be going to the Channel five emergency broadcasting system. Please stay tuned to your local A.M Radio stations. Thank you. And, good luck to everyone."

(Andrew gets up, takes out his earpiece, and walks away from his desk. The desk sits, empty for a moment. The screen switches to a logo reading 'CHANNEL FIVE EMERGENCY BROADCASTING STATION' and a 'no service' tone.)
FADE TO BLACK.

PETER

That was it… This broken news has revealed that a virus has begun sweeping through the country, and it looks as if it began somewhere in New England. The lack of knowledge presented in the interviews and various news segments was absolutely terrifying. It sounds as if the people infected with the sickness are actually considered dead. I don't know what to think about that… It doesn't seem real—it couldn't seem real.

It appears as if the government has been doing all they can to keep things together, but the whole thing seems too big, too surreal. They've asked Canada and Mexico to construct safe zones. It has only been a couple of days and they expect it to spread that far? It makes me wonder if they'll be able to contain it or if the

President and everyone else just said that to make those listening feel a little better.

We could be here for a long time, I feel…

THIN HOPE

PETER

It had been a couple of days since the last news broadcast. We've hooked up an A.M. radio and have been monitoring it ever since. Other than a pre-recorded message reading off the safe zones listed on the news, we have heard nothing. We raided the paint section of the store today. Jen and Tara began painting some large tarps which we will try to hang from the roof. Samantha is working with them too, but Jen told me she hasn't been doing much of anything — just sitting and being real quiet, barely saying a word all day. I suppose no one can blame her as she has taken the loss of Robbie very badly. I haven't taken much time to sit and think about it, but then again, I'm still here with Jen and any other thinking I've been doing has been about my mom and if she's okay. The last we heard, Canada had set up safe zones, but there was no infection.

While the girls readied signs for the roof, I pointed Mike in the direction of incoming stock. I knew from my past experience working here for Robbie's dad, that a lot of new stock comes in at the beginning of the summer and I wondered if there would be anything useful — especially camping gear and whatnot. While I watched from the window, Mike was opening more boxes than a kid on Christmas, trying to find anything of use.

Also, I found half a dozen flare guns packed in automotive *crash kits*. We decided to keep one with us at all times in case a helicopter flies overhead—which has yet to happen. I keep thinking I'm hearing one off in the distance, but it's likely my imagination.

After the broadcast went off the air, we decided to pull our resources. We filled jugs of water from the tap to save in case the water shuts off or becomes unsanitary—Mike's idea. Also, we raided the office and vending machines.

We got dozens of cans of soda and a box full of candies and snacks—everything from M&M's to Hog Lumps. We also gathered first aid kits in case of any injuries. However, the injury we are all trying to avoid would not be cured by some gauze, salt sniffers or Band-Aids. The hardware store was shaping up to be a pretty well-stocked shelter for this small group of people, but one thing we didn't have was gasoline.

There were bottles of oil in the automotive section, but in accordance with Massachusetts law, we couldn't have gas in the store. We all agreed that gasoline was a must-have for the car Tara brought here. There are many reasons the car may come in handy. For instance, if we needed to leave it would be a hell of a lot quicker if we had a working vehicle. Tara has claimed that the car is in good working order and is also pretty fast—perfect for our situation.

Also, gasoline would be a necessity for the small generators that the store sold. If we lost power, the generators would be a huge help, especially if we ever came across food that would benefit from being heated.

Soon enough, Mike came from the stock room holding some boxes—motion sensor lights. Earlier, he'd asked me if I thought the store either had any security cameras or sold anything that could work.

I told him it wasn't likely. Robbie's dad had *cameras* installed that would face the register, but the thing is—they're fake. They are in plain sight and I guess his hope was that the idea of surveillance would simply deter any thieves from robbing the store. So, Mike presented the idea of motion sensor lights as a makeshift security system at night… If any of them stumble in our direction, we would see them coming.

However, Mike and I shared the same concern about the idea. If one or two were walking near the store and set off the lights, would a dozen from down the street notice and create a bigger problem? We decided to put them aside and possibly talk to everyone else and come up with some sort of idea.

JEN

Tara and I finished making a large sign on some twelve foot square paint tarps. We took black paint and wrote 'HELP' and 'SOS' on the tarps. Soon, a couple of us will attempt to get them onto the roof. Peter and Robbie put a big sale sign up there once, they said it was a pain to do, but we had confidence that we'd be able to get it done. Tara seemed like a very nice and competent girl. She seemed sad about all that has happened, but we've been keeping ourselves busy and that seems to be helping her cope with—or perhaps avoid—her problems.

Also, Mike and Peter have been talking about getting some gasoline to keep in canisters if we need it. I think it's a good idea, but I don't know about them walking down the street half a mile to the nearest gas station.

Their plan seems to be taking some gas cans sold here at the store in a couple shopping carts and just fill them up. However, Mike was concerned that the pumps would be off and they would have to find a way to override the system or something. He was also concerned that people may have come and looted the gas already.

Peter doubted that though, using the rationale that if there were looters in the area, they probably would've come here for the *weapons*, tools, and other supplies.

Eventually, Peter and Mike gathered us together and asked who wanted to go onto the roof to put up the sign. Peter said he would go with one other person to help him—since he had actually gone up there before. Mike offered to stay here and keep a look out by the front window.

So, I offered to go up with Pete. Tara would help Mike by just being available to let us know if anything happens—that being said, we will be on the roof and may even see things before Mike. Throughout all of this, Sam had retreated to the backroom again; I don't think she's sleeping, probably just lying there thinking—or not thinking.

Next, Peter and I grabbed the tarps and various supplies to hang up on the roof—tape, hooks, zip-ties, etc. We were also bringing our flare guns as we decided we could wait up there after hanging the signs and attempt to flag over any rescue crews, should we see anyone in the skies or off in the distance.

MIKE

Tara and I waited by the front display window of the store as Jen and Peter went up to the roof to hang the signs. We sat with our arsenal of weapons in case of any A. Phagy carriers stumbling into our area.

I was curious about what Tara had been through—but I didn't want to pry. However, after sitting in silence for a while, she began to tell me how her boyfriend had run away from his car and she found it abandoned.

She seemed broken up, yet hopeful that he's alive somewhere. I let her hold onto that thin hope as I told her that he's probably okay—even though I was sure he was now walking the streets with the rest of the infected. This made me a little upset as I thought about how others would probably think that about my Ellie.

But, it was different... Her mother took her to the safe zone once this thing was reported. They weren't running around the town somewhere like Tara's man was. I had to cling to this idea.

Soon, we began to hear a noise coming from above us. At first, it startled me as the sound was so unfamiliar. Then, Tara said, "It sounds like they made it up to the roof..."

I felt a little stupid. Of course it was them walking on the roof. I guess the idea of what we were looking outside for has skewed my judgment a little. Nonetheless, they had made it onto the roof which means we're halfway there.

As Tara told me about her boyfriend, I couldn't help but think of nothing other than my daughter. I'm sure what she's going through is terrible, but I just can't imagine losing Ellie—this is something I simply will not accept. We're getting out of here and I am going to find her.

I began thinking about Pete and Jen on the roof, affixing the signs and using the flares to flag down a helicopter or maybe some National Guard transport vehicle patrolling through town.

Suddenly, my day dreaming was cut short as I heard Tara gasp at the sight of half-a-dozen infected creeps stumbling in our direction several yards away in the street.

"What should we do?" she asked me.

"They must see Peter and Jen up there," I explained. "We should warn them!"

"I'll go," she said as she ran to the stairs in the back.

I stood and watched the ghouls for a second as they stumbled alongside one another, seemingly with purpose. I grabbed the gun and a large shovel as I continued watching them for a moment, hoping they would turn and start in another direction. No such luck.

They walked with an intent I hadn't seen before. There was no question, they had noticed Peter and Jen on the roof and they had begun their deathly pursuit.

As I noticed the sound of frantic steps—Tara likely running onto the roof, I decided to head out there and try to take out the infected. Wielding a shovel and a shotgun, I quickly unlocked the door and headed in their direction.

PETER

We had attached one of the signs using zip-ties to some old rusty hooks that had been used to set up the sales signs in a more normal time. Suddenly, as we worked on getting the second sign up, Tara came running onto the roof, almost slipping on the slightly slanted tile.

"There's a bunch…" Tara began before Jen cut off her screaming, "*Look!*"

We all stared out at the parking lot and witnessed six infected people staggering in our direction—one even reaching its bloody and pale arm our way. Then, Mike came running out of the store with some gear in his hands.

"Mike!" I shouted to him.

"He went out?" Tara asked excitedly.

Mike paid no mind to our screaming as he approached the closest one and swung the shovel like a baseball bat—collapsing it's skull into its brain. The remaining undead all set their sights on Mike after this and began coming towards him from all sides. I began to yell nonsense at the undead, trying to take their focus off of Mike. I was on a roof and they weren't going to be able to reach me whereas Mike was in a much more vulnerable position. However, this didn't seem to be working, they had their lifeless eyes fixated on Mike and were not going to stop.

Mike raised the gun, ready to shoot, as we looked on helplessly and anxiously. I really hoped we wouldn't have to use the shells, but I'd rather be out of ammo than have Mike become lunch for these monsters.

Their dried lips curled over their gnashing teeth as they stumbled towards Mike, boxing him in. Mike fidgeted around, trying to find an exit route as he put down the gun and raised the bloody shovel once again.

Suddenly, Tara took off, running back down the stairs. Jen tried to stop her to no avail. I didn't know what she planned on doing, but whatever it was, she moved with some serious intent.

Mike made a break for it, running through a small gap between two of the infected hosts. He ran towards the store, leveling one of the creeps with the shovel, not killing it, but knocking it to the ground.

After creating some space between himself and the infected, he turned around and swung the shovel hard at one infected person's head. Dark crimson splattered everywhere as he crashed the edge of the shovel through the ghoul's face.

He then made his way to the store where Tara opened the front door and said, "Hurry!" He ran until he looked back and noticed the shotgun lying in the middle of the lot. "Shit! The shotgun!" he yelled.

"Get it later!"

"No, we'll need it if more start showing up!" he told Tara.

He turned back towards the parking lot only to be greeted by the one he had previously knocked down. He brought the shovel down to its face, similar to how a javelin sticks into the ground.

At this point, three more infected people were honing in on Mike. As one lunged towards him, he took care of it swiftly with the shovel. Then, the other two came rather quickly in his direction simultaneously.

He turned quickly and swung the shovel once more. It smashed one of the infected right in the side of the head and ended its undead existence. However, as he delivered the blow, the shovel slipped from his grasp and flew several feet away.

The last of this herd of infected was coming at him fast until, out of nowhere, a flare from close proximity exploded into the side of the ghoul's head. It fell to the ground with the lit flare as Tara stood there holding her flare gun nervously.

Mike quickly picked up the gun and left the blood-covered shovel, then ran towards the store, past the scattered and battered bodies strewn about the parking lot. "Thank you," he said to Tara.

"No problem," she said as she rushed back into the store.

At this point, Jen and I had gone back downstairs and met them inside.

"Are you guys okay?" I asked immediately.

They both nodded as Tara dropped the empty flare gun in disgust at the whole situation.

"That was close," Mike said. "Are the signs up?"

"All up," I told him. "Now we wait."

He nodded and looked out the window at the sky.

TYPICAL PROTOCOL

JEN

About a week had gone by since we put the signs on the roof. There have been no air traffic whatsoever, nor have there been any signs of vehicles on the street. We've been taking turns waiting at the window, listening and looking at nothing but random infected people walking by the store and the clouds.

You'd think such a calm and clear sky would be relaxing, but it has become quite unnerving just hoping and praying for anything to fly overhead. Mike and Pete were comparing it to the week following 9/11 when all air traffic was suspended. The difference between then and now is I remember being scared if I heard a plane or helicopter. Now, I pray that I'll hear one. Also, we have heard absolutely no chatter at all on the AM radio…I'm starting to get a sense that we're going to be here for the long haul at this point.

It was about eight in the morning; I had been sitting at the front window for a couple of hours. Tara and Samantha were still sleeping in the back—this was basically all Sam had been doing as of late.

Mike and Pete were in the back sorting through some useful merchandise they found—not sure what it is, but I'm crossing my fingers for food as we've basically been living off of snacks lately and we're just about out of the instant coffee, which, even though it tastes horrible, is about the best treat we've had.

It had rained for a couple of days earlier in the week and the puddles in the parking lot were tinted red from the diseased bodies still laying and decaying on the gravel.

After the rain stopped and the blood had mostly washed away, Mike, Pete and I put on those large yellow gloves, some paint aprons, and removed the bodies. We moved them to a patch of tall grass and weeds just beyond the lot. It was disgusting, most of their heads were smashed in and the blood had washed away so they almost looked like people again, with very pale and dried out skin.

Also, their eyes were blank with a whitish/gray tint to them... It looked as if they wouldn't be able to see, but who knows. Many of them had bite marks on their arms, neck, and shoulder areas. The marks were grossly infected with a gray tinge to them and dark red—almost black—vein marks stemming from the wound for several inches until they faded into the lifeless skin.

Tara came from the back room. "Morning," I said to her. She simply waved as she made her way over to sit with me. She appeared to have a blank look on her face, but it was hard to tell if something was wrong or if she was still half-asleep. "Is everything okay?" I asked. A tear ran down her cheek as she shrugged and looked out the window.

"I'm just...I'm just never going to see him again," she answered.

I rubbed her back as I told her, "You don't know that."

She shook her head, "I do. I do know that and so do you."

I did know that, but I didn't want to say that to her. I couldn't even bring myself to say it to Sam about Robbie, even though we did know that for a fact.

She then told me it was her birthday tomorrow. I felt terrible that she had to spend it this way. At the same time, I was surprised she even knew the date as I'd lost track sometime last week. It was still June—that's all I knew. Poor girl.

Suddenly, Mike and Pete emerged from the stock room with smiles on their faces. "Good news!" Pete said, happily.

"What happened?" I asked.

"We found some good stuff," Mike explained.

"Sam's on her way out," Pete said. "We'll tell all of you together."

Soon, Sam came out from the back room looking mentally exhausted, but also curious about what was going on. She walked over and I gave her my seat.

"Hey, Sam," I said.

She looked up at me and attempted to smile, but couldn't seem to produce one. I rubbed her back and looked over to Mike and Pete.

Mike placed a large box on the cashier's counter next to a smaller box that Pete had placed there. Mike began to open the large box as Pete looked through the small one that was already opened.

"We're running low on food that we've recovered from the office and vending machines," Pete said. "However, Mike and I found some very useful items in a big camping pallet of stock that was just sitting there in the back."

Mike pulled out a white packet from the large box and said, "Voila! Chicken Parm!"

"What?" I asked anxiously.

"Dehydrated food!" Peter yelled.

"Seriously?" I asked again, overjoyed.

"That stuff will last a long time," Tara said.

"For sure. Unfortunately, we have a limited supply," Pete replied.

"How many?"

"A dozen packets," Mike said.

"Yeah," Pete chimed in. "Mike and I were talking and we're doing okay right now, but we could really use some more supplies."

"All right..." I replied cautiously.

"If we head out soon, we can make it to the gas station and back before dark."

"You're going to have to walk there?" I asked.

Pete looked at Mike and nodded.

I shook my head. "I don't think it's a good idea."

"We'll be okay," Mike insisted.

"What about what happened when we put up the signs?" I asked angrily.

"We'll go fast, not staying in one place too long," Pete said. "And we'll have the gun and some other tools with us."

Suddenly, Mike quickly ran to the back room and said, "I forgot something!"

He returned, holding a small plastic package. "Look, we can use these!" he said.

He handed the item to Pete; it was a set of walkie-talkies with a range of five miles. These were a Godsend for our situation.

PETER

Mike and I began getting things together for our little expedition to the gas station. It was weird; I had been to this gas station dozens of times without giving it a second thought. But, now our whole day would be centered on getting there and back without any problems.

We loaded up a couple of shopping carts with one and two-gallon canisters that would be used to collect the gasoline. At the same time, Jen and Tara figured out how to use the walkies so we could all keep in touch. Also, we gathered up a couple of shovels—which was becoming our go-to *weapon* throughout all of this—and the shotgun.

The gas station would be about a half a mile away from the hardware store. If we left now and didn't have any problems at all, we would return a little after noon at the latest. However, I fully expected us to hit a few speed bumps along the road.

Soon, Jen came up to me and gave me a brief lesson on how to use the walkie-talkie, instructing me to leave it on channel two at all times, and make sure to wait one second after I press the button to speak. I could tell she was ecstatic at the idea of being able to reach us. I have to admit, I was pretty fond of the idea myself.

So, after loading up our gear, we got ready to go and decided we would test out the walkies every couple buildings to make sure we didn't lose the signal or anything.

Jen ran up to me as we approached the doors and hugged me for a long time—like something out of an epic war movie when the girl hugs the guy as he is about to head into battle. The streets were clear so I hoped we weren't heading into any kind of a battle.

Mike was getting quiet but didn't seem too nervous. I tried to focus on the task at hand and not think about what was happening. Thinking about everything, I came to realize that I was more nervous that the pumps wouldn't work or would be empty than I was about the threat of infection. We had gotten away from the infected before, we could do it again.

Mike finally stepped out of the store and into the empty lot. I could still see dark marks of blood stained pavement where the corpses were before we moved them. The spots looked more like dirt or oil stains at this point, but it was still quite disturbing to think of what was actually there.

Jen shut and locked the door behind us. She and Tara would wait by the window until we returned. Mike and I looked back at them for a moment—then to each other. Then, we began pushing our shopping carts through the lot; they were loud on the rough pavement. I didn't think about this and definitely became a little nervous that the undead would surely be able to hear us. Luckily, the road was much smoother than the old pavement at Fix-It and made them a little quieter.

As we reached the road, the walkie-talkie beeped and Jen's voice came through the light static ambience. "Good luck," she said. I looked back at the store and they were staring at us through the window. I simply gave them a thumb's up and kept going.

"Do you think we'll come across any of them?" Mike asked.

"Probably," I said. "But they're slow. Hopefully we can avoid any close combat."

Mike nodded and asked, "You nervous?"

I shrugged. "Not as much as I thought I'd be. I'm just crossing my fingers that we won't have any problems actually getting the gas."

"We may have to turn on the power depending upon if the attendant shut it off before this all happened."

"Do you know how?" I asked.

"I've never done it before," Mike explained. "But we can figure it out."

We continued down the road which wasn't too bad looking. A couple of cars were abandoned along the side, one had its windshield broken and the inside was stained with blood. However, there was no sign of an occupant. There was no sign of any infected as far as we could see on the road.

However, we did pass a vacuum service shop where we witnessed a male and female with employee shirts and nametags on, scraping and pounding against the blood stained front window. They appeared to have been locked in when they became infected. At this point, it was safe to say that these too would spend the rest of their existence—or undead existence—inside that shop, trying to get out.

As we passed the vacuum repair shop, Mike looked at me and said, "Well, that sucks."

After a moment, I started to chuckle at the terrible joke, as did Mike. It was then that I realized how desensitized we had become and that two weeks ago, I would've thought that was a terrible thing to say. I felt that Mike was thinking the same thing.

We didn't dwell too much on it and continued moving. The road we were walking on soon turned into a hill for a while, so it was getting a little tiring pushing the carts. We tried not to stop as I told Mike that the gas station was only a little further after we reached the top of the hill.

Eventually, we reached the top of the hill and could barely see the sign for the gas station off in the distance. We stopped for a moment and I decided to try the walkie to let Jen and Tara know of our position.

I held down the button for a moment and said, "Hey, guys."

I waited for a moment until Jen's voice came back and said, "Peter?"

"We're almost at the gas station," I said. "Things have been pretty quiet."

As I said this, I should've knocked on wood because all of a sudden, a pair of undead came stumbling from between two buildings.

One knocked over a trash can as it lunged towards us. Luckily the trash can caused it to trip and gave us an opportunity to move away from them. We backed away from them, keeping the shopping carts in front of us, hoping we might be able to push them away if needed.

The other undead individual stumbled around the trash can and its counterpart and came towards us slowly. I engaged in what I am now referring to as *typical protocol* and brought my shovel to the disease carrier's head. At the same time, the one who had fallen began to get up. While it was on all fours, Mike charged directly at it with his cart. It didn't kill it, but it pushed the infected back and tangled its arm in the undercarriage of the shopping cart. It was really stuck in there as Mike attempted to back away from it; its body tumbled along with the cart, flailing painfully on the ground and knocking trash all over the place.

"Shit," Mike said as he shook his cart from side to side, trying to shake the grimacing ghoul loose. The sickly thing gnashed its teeth at us and growled as it kept trying to steady itself on the ground.

I picked up the trashcan and slammed the bottom down onto the head of the infected. It also didn't kill it, but it slowed it down considerably. Mike then tugged the cart quickly and the arm came loose.

The creep then rolled to the side on the ground and mumbled some gargling noises as it tried to find its undead equilibrium. Mike took the shovel from me and took it upon himself to engage in *typical protocol*.

After the commotion, we could see a couple of moving figures several blocks away. We weren't a hundred percent sure if they knew we were there, but we decided to not wait around to find out. We quickly continued on our path to regular, unleaded treasure.

JOEY

It was dark inside and I hadn't seen anyone since my arrival, nor had I seen any of the sick ones walking around in at least a few days. Perhaps things were calming down or maybe they were finally succumbing to the disease. Who knows?

I was surrounded by empty water and soda bottles, as well as empty bags of nut mixes, chips and pretzel bags. Things had grown repetitive and I had lost the will to constantly be looking out the windows for people. Truthfully, I began to lose the will to live. I was pretty sure my family, friends, and girlfriend were all dead and I knew no help was coming. This was the stage I never thought would come: acceptance.

Upon arriving, I hadn't planned on staying. After all, who would think about living in a gas station? But, it just happened - plenty of snacks and a shotgun to boot. I located a box of shotgun shells and taught myself how to load the gun. I shot it once about a week ago, just to make sure I did it right. I took one of their heads clean off.

Usually they stumble past the station, sometimes stepping on the bell-cords hard enough to set the bell off. When this happens, they typically stumble around for a while, looking for someone or something—too stupid or primitive enough to realize that they caused the sound. Half the time, I end up having to deal with them because they either somehow detect me or some instinct lands them at the door and they pound away for ages.

One night, it happened right as it got dark. I knew it couldn't see me so I just left it. It sat there slapping the door with its bloody mitts relentlessly until morning when I finally dealt with it—this was my shotgun test.

Typically, they just wander by without paying any mind to the station or the fact that I'm inside. The first day here, I counted forty-three from the sunrise until I finally fell asleep behind the counter. I arrived here after running for miles the night that every-thing happened, and I've been here ever since. It's almost time to go though—one way or the other.

Suddenly, I heard some kind of noise, a noise I certainly had not heard since I'd been here. I couldn't tell what it was so I had to look out the window. To my surprise it was two guys pushing a couple shopping carts towards the pumps. They looked fine— definitely not sick. One had a gun and the other had a blood stained shovel. There was no telling if these guys were friendly or what. They pulled up to the pumps and each took gas canisters out of the carts. I crouched down as low as I could and silently watched them... They had no idea I was there.

I continued watching them as they pumped gas and surveyed the area. The door was locked and they had no reason not to smash it open and look for supplies. I grew nervous at the idea of dealing with anyone, so nervous that I set aside the thought that they might be able to get me out of here. I had really been here too long.

Soon enough, one of them finished filling his canisters and began walking towards the door. I crawled into a space below the counter and clutched the shotgun as tight as I could. I heard him walk to the door and try to open it. "It's locked!" he shouted to his friend.

"So what," his friend replied. "We got the gas. Let's head back."

"Are you sure we shouldn't just check inside?"

"Do you think we can get in?"

"The door is glass... It can't be too difficult with that shovel."

I grew extremely anxious at the idea of these two looters coming in. I double checked the shotgun to make sure it was loaded and actually began to pray. I didn't want to shoot anyone—I also didn't want anyone to shoot me. It's funny; I was ready for everything to be over, but with this staring me in the face, I just wanted everything to be okay. I guess if it ends, I want it to be on my own terms.

Suddenly, I heard a smash from the outside. My world seemed to shake as I did my best to sit still. Then, I heard another noise, followed by a shatter. They broke the door and in turn broke my situation. Even if they didn't find me, I'd be forced to leave as the store would no longer be secure.

"I can't believe you just did that," the seemingly more cautious one said.

"I know, I never thought I'd break into a store before."

"Look at all the wrappers on the ground. Do you think someone was here?"

I heard them stepping around the register... They were going to find me; I clutched my gun even tighter than before.

"It looks like it," the one who shattered the door said.

"Do you see anything of use?"

"Just snacks and drinks."

"Anything you like?"

"I don't know. Maybe some of these energy bars."

I started feeling a little less anxious. They didn't sound malicious, but I couldn't pop out at them at this point. As far as I knew, one was still holding a gun. I didn't want to test any theories so I decided to sit tight and wait until they left.

One sounded like he grabbed some energy bars and the other made a comment about all the unscratched scratch tickets above the register, how there could be a million dollars sitting there. I remembered thinking the same thing, but I guess it didn't matter now. The question was would it ever matter again?

Soon enough, they left the store and went back to their shopping carts now full of gas. I waited until I heard the sound of the carts rolling until I looked back out. I watched them leave the station together.

I waited for a moment as I stared at the shattered door. I couldn't stay here. I let them have some distance and decided to follow them and see where they were headed.

MIKE

After a pretty successful trip to the gas station, Peter and I headed back to the hardware store. Peter radioed over to Jen and told her our status, reporting that we got twenty-seven gallons of gasoline. The bill was a total of $109.33. That almost made me glad that we were in a situation where the economy wasn't relevant.

We both remembered the crowds of undead we saw a few blocks away as we headed back down the hill cautiously. We went as slow as possible while the fully loaded shopping carts pulled us down the slant.

While we moved quickly down the hill, we both noticed one infected person stumbling in front of a store a few buildings down from the vacuum place. Since it was only one, we decided to keep going and just get back to the hardware store and gas up Tara's car.

As we continued down the street, we noticed a lot of papers and trash being blown around by the wind; this was from the infected that knocked over the trashcan earlier in the day. Other than the one we passed earlier, we didn't see much of anything. So, we kept going as fast as possible until we heard a gunshot from somewhere behind us.

We both dropped to ours knees in fear that someone might have been shooting at us. I began wondering if we looted the wrong gas station. I thought that maybe the owner was held up in the store and we just pissed him off.

We both crouched behind our shopping carts and looked down the road. We couldn't see anyone anywhere. After a moment, we decided to keep going even faster than before.

I explained my theory of the pissed off gas station owner to Peter and he seemed nervous about the idea. We both agreed that if this was the case, we would try to reason with him and work it out. I began to worry that we might lose the gas after all that trouble. Then, I started thinking about how I broke the door. If my theory was correct the guy must have been really pissed off.

After booking it nonstop to Fix-It and even ignoring a call from Jen, we finally arrived and Jen saw us immediately. She ran to the door and unlocked it right away. Neither of us liked the idea of so much gas being inside the building, so we parked the shopping carts on the side of the building.

"How'd everything go?" Jen asked as she let us in.

"It went okay," Peter said as we entered the store.

I shut the door and locked it behind us as Jen inquired about Peter's *tone.*

I chimed in. "We heard a gunshot on the way back. We think someone may have been following us."

"We'll just have to keep a low profile," Peter suggested.

I nodded in agreement as Tara and Samantha came out of the back room.

"So, you got gas for the car?" Tara asked.

"Yeah," Peter said. "We'll take it out in a couple days to the grocery store and get some real supplies."

Peter and I sat for a while by the window, waiting for someone to come by. As it started to get dark, we decided to go gas up the car. We both agreed that if someone did come for the gas, at least we would have some in the car.

We told Jen who decided to wait with Sam by the window while we were out there. She insisted we take the shotgun in case anyone did show up. For the first time, we were looking out for a person—not the undead, which was still a concern in itself.

So, we brought one of the shopping carts over to the car and began filling up the tank one canister at a time. While Peter did that, I checked the glove compartment to see if the car had a manual. It did, so I looked up how big the tank was—eleven gallons. This way, we didn't have to accidentally go over and waste any gas spilling out on the ground.

Eventually, we got the car just about filled up and started it to make sure the battery hadn't died. Everything was ready to go, so we once again hid the rest of the gasoline around the side of the building and headed back inside.

There wasn't any sign of movement anywhere outside. It had become dark and I began wondering if all the undead in the area would've been drawn to the gun shot we heard. Perhaps whoever it was...was already dead.

JEN

The sun had begun to rise and Peter had recently fallen asleep by the front window. We took turns watching it last night and he was out like a light a couple of hours before dawn.

Mike, Tara and Sam were all asleep in the back. I think Mike and Peter were very tired after yesterday's trip. The walk wasn't too long, but I couldn't imagine how mentally exhausting it must have been to be on edge every second with no real shelter or anything. They said they came across a few undead out there, but nothing too crazy. It must have been so strange—especially for Peter because this was where he grew up—to see the streets in the state they're in.

Suddenly, I looked across the parking lot and saw a man holding a shotgun, walking towards the car. He was around our age and looked pretty beaten up and worn down. Immediately, I shook Peter and said, "Wake up!" He woke, startled and confused. I then pointed out the window. "I think the gas station owner is here," I said.

Peter and I watched for a moment as the man walked around the car and began looking around the store. We sat motionless and were pretty sure he couldn't see us.

Peter slowly grabbed the gun. "I'm going to see what he wants," he said.

I tried to tell him not to but he stood up and went to the door.

He unlocked the door. The man immediately looked directly at Peter and raised his gun. Peter stepped outside and quickly pointed the gun at this man. "Take it easy," Peter said sternly yet nervously.

"You're the one from the gas station," the man said.

Peter looked at him for a moment before responding, "Listen, we needed that gas. I'm sorry."

The man stared at Peter for a second and lowered his gun. He then looked over at the car. "This is my car," he said.

Peter shook his head and kept the gun on the man. "No way, man."

Suddenly, before I even realized she came from the back room, Tara ran past me and through the front door. She ran at the seemingly crazed man and wrapped her arms around him.

"What the hell?" Peter said softly.

The man dropped his gun and hugged Tara as tears ran down his face covered in shock.

"I can't believe you're here," Tara said.

Peter looked back at me in the window with a confused look on his face as I began to realize that this must be Tara's boyfriend. But how was that possible?

After a moment, Peter turned around and came inside. "Is that..." he began to say.

"Her boyfriend, I think," I told him.

"Makes sense now," Peter said. "He said it was his car. He must've been held up in the gas station."

"What are the odds?" I asked. "And, today's Tara's birthday." I chuckled in amazement at the strange situation.

After a long hug, he picked up his gun and they both came inside the store.

"This is Joey. My boyfriend," Tara said.

"Sorry about that," Peter said.

"No problem," Joey replied. "I had no idea who you and your friend were at the gas station, so I just hid behind the counter…"

Mike walked out of the backroom and stared at Joey with confusion as he asked, "What the hell is going on?"

TARA

It was the only thing I wanted for my birthday, to see Joey again. I was almost in shock when I saw him in the parking lot and I still couldn't believe it as we stood in the store together. Mike and Peter laughed as he told them about thinking they were violent looters at the gas station.

He also said that he was angry at first when Mike smashed the door to his shelter, but if he hadn't there would've been no reason to follow them back here. At this point, I thanked Mike for breaking the door. He said it was an *enjoyable experience*.

Eventually, Joey gave Mike his shotgun and they sorted through that and the box of ammo he had brought with him. Everyone seemed quite pleased with having another gun. After that, Joey and I went into the office while the rest of them stayed by the window.

When we entered the office, I poured him one of the last cups of lukewarm coffee we were able to conjure up. Joey loved it. He has always liked that simple crappy coffee, while I've preferred more flavorful fair-trade products. Regardless, I was very happy to give it to him after what he had been through.

Then, he went straight to the TV, turned it on, and began flipping through the channels of static. "Did you guys ever see anything on here?" he asked frantically.

"We watched some news until they went off the air a while ago," I explained.

He looked at me for a moment and, eventually and impatiently, asked, "Well, what's happening?"

"You haven't heard anything?"

"No," he exclaimed.

Shocked at the aspect of uncertainty he must've been suffering through this whole time, I sat down and explained everything we knew—the Arthriphagy virus, the safe zones, the timeline of how it had spread, everything…

After a while of sitting together and talking, he told me what had happened to him the night he disappeared. And, I told him what we had been through. I somewhat explained what had happened with Peter, Jen, Sam and Mike too.

Eventually, Jen knocked on the door and asked if we could join them. So, we headed out to the store where everyone was sitting by the window and cash register. Joey got his first look at Sam and I could tell he saw the distress she was going through.

Joey and I sat with the group and we all discussed a plan. Jen then walked away without saying anything. Then, Peter began by saying, "Okay, we have some good supplies and now that we have some gas in the car, we have to go get some food and anything else useful from the grocery store. Now, I am volunteering to go. I'd like to have one other person with me to help."

Mike raised his hand. "I'll go."

Peter nodded and looked at Joey. "It's your car I guess…"

Immediately, I objected. "No! He's not going, not now."

"I think I'd rather sit this one out," Joey said, much more calmly than I.

"That's fine," Peter said. "Just wanted to offer."

Then, Jen came back holding a packet of food and a plastic fork. The smell was cheap—but amazing. She then handed it to me. "You can kick off our dehydrated food supply by trying out this Chicken Parm. Happy birthday!" she said.

I smiled as I took the warm packet from her and smelled the food for a moment. "Thank you so much," I said.

Then Peter put a piece of paper on the cashier's counter. "We need to come up with a shopping list," he said.

PETER

There I was, walking into this small diner, with clean and brightly colored walls and décor. I walked to a booth where Jen, Sam and Robbie were sitting, looking at menus. Robbie's face was buried in his menu and if it wasn't for his Fix-It shirt, I might not have even known it was him!

As I sat down, I looked to the bar where Mike and his daughter were sitting. Mike was feeding her pancakes and he nodded to me when I saw them. Ellie had her back to me though, so I didn't say hi. Then, Tara walked by with a tray of waters and quickly greeted us but continued on her way because she had her own tables to wait. I watched her walk to her section and began to chuckle when I saw Joey wiping down her tables—he was the busboy?

After having a good chuckle at the irony, I began looking at the menu and the first thing that caught my eye was a cheeseburger. Now that sounded good!

"I'm definitely getting a burger!" I said aloud.

At this point, the waitress came to our table. The light hanging over our table blocked my view of her face so it was kind of awkward, but I ordered my burger and she immediately handed one to me and said in a cheerful tone, "Enjoy!"

I was delighted as I looked at the juicy burger and fries. Then, I bit into it and pulled it away from my mouth quickly. The inside of the burger was bleeding like a gaping wound and had little maggots crawling around the inside.

It smelled terrible and I dropped it on the table as quickly as possible. "Is something wrong with your meal?" I heard the waitress ask. Then, I looked up and her face came out from behind the light fixture and revealed a rotting and wrinkly undead face with tons of makeup on—like she was trying to hide the fact that she was infected.

"What the hell!" I said, shocked.

Robbie then lowered his menu to reveal the same type of look as our waitress. Needless to say, I stood up and tried to back out of the restaurant as they came towards me. Then, Mike, Ellie, Sam, Joey and Tara joined them as they all appeared to be walking corpses.

"Jen!" I shouted.

She looked over and revealed that she too had been infected. Was I alone? What happened?

I immediately opened my eyes and felt as if I could taste the rotten meat from my terrible dream. This felt like one of those dreams that were going to stick with me for a while. The thought of everyone I was with currently—including Jen—trying to eat me was not something I enjoyed waking up to.

Despite all of the terrifying aspects I had endured, I kept thinking of the sight of the nice fresh burger and realized how much I wanted some real food. I guess it was a good thing we were going to the grocery store today. The thought of food got me up and out of bed quickly—anything to think of something other than the horrible dream I had.

We spent last night making a list for the grocery store, talking, eating small portions of Tara's chicken parmesan, and relaxing as well. We got to know Joey a bit too—he seemed like a real cool guy.

Once again, Mike and I prepared to venture out this morning, taking a trip about four times as long as our last one. This time, however, we have the car, two guns, a walkie-talkie, and an enlightened hope that there may be others out there.

As we looked over our list, it was safe to say that we were both feeling pretty good about our mission ahead of us.

The list we all compiled was broken down into three groups: essentials, non-edible essentials, and finally treats—non essentials that we certainly wouldn't risk our lives for, but if we had space and could easily grab the item or items, we would.

SHOPPING LIST
1) Essentials
Bottled water
Canned soups, beans, etc.
Cereal

2) Non-edible
OTC meds
Wet naps
Hand sanitizer
Anti-biotics

3) Others – not essential
Long lasting snack foods
Shampoo/soap

Toothpaste
INSTANT COFFEE***

As we prepared, Joey checked the shotguns and discovered they both took the same size shells. We had about two dozen, not an indispensable amount, but much better than the few we had before.

So, we split the ammo equally between Mike and me. Then, we armed ourselves with shovels in case of some typical protocol. We gathered the rest of our necessities for the trip and loaded the car.

After loading the car, Jen approached me and asked, "Are you nervous this time?"

I shook my head confidently. "No way. If we were able to make that gas station trip, we'll be fine with another gun and a car."

She didn't look at me and simply rubbed my back for a moment and said, "Just be careful."

As she walked away, I began to feel that I was acting a little overconfident as we looked ahead to this trip. After all, Joey was near us this whole time, no one here had been as far as the grocery store.

We had no idea what things looked like there. Her little pep talk made me realize that we would have to go into this trip expecting the unexpected and keeping our guard up. I think we both still felt confident, but we weren't going to lose our surroundings.

MIKE

Peter and I piled our things into the car as Joey stood outside with us. It was a cloudy morning as we prepared to leave. Though, it was hard to tell if it was going to be a rainy or stormy day.

This would certainly add an extra element to our planning for the day.

I observed the gray sky and smelled the air, searching for that scent of incoming rain. Jen and Tara joined their significant others by the car.

Tara immediately latched herself onto Joey. I can't blame her... If Ellie was here, I don't think I'd let go of her for a second. Joey's safe arrival had given me new hope that Ellie was alive. She has to be.

Peter then gave Jen a hug and kiss in such a way that I knew we were leaving.

I hopped in the passenger's seat as Peter was far more familiar with the area than I was. A moment later, Peter grabbed Joey's keys and got in the car. Jen came up to the car. "Be careful you guys," she said.

We both nodded and said we would as Peter put the key in the ignition and started the engine. Then, we proceeded to slowly pull the car out of the parking lot, taking it pretty slow as the car had sat idle for quite some time.

Jen, Tara and Joey watched us for a moment as we drove away from Fix-It. Then, they turned around and headed back into the store. As we continued on route, the skies worsened and a fog started to settle in.

I could finally see the incoming rain as I started to search for a button that would cover the roof of the convertible. The interior had been enduring the weather since it was parked at the store originally so it wasn't a huge deal. But, the cover would keep us from getting wet—and while I wasn't scared of rain, I did want to keep from catching a cold which would greatly exacerbate the situation.

However, Peter caught me looking around curiously and pressed a button. As the collapsible roof began to extend over our heads, he said, "Was this what you were looking for?"

I laughed. "Yes, thank you."

We continued on our way as the fog greatly thickened and it seemed to become much darker outside. Peter turned on the lights—high beams and all. Soon, we drove beyond the area of the gas station and into the previously unknown territory.

Things looked no different—abandoned cars, trash and various items strewn about, and some bodies lying in the road. Many bodies had been picked apart as if a vulture had feasted on them for dinner.

Moments later, I found out my thoughts were correct about the picked apart bodies as we came upon several vultures ripping apart a corpse in the road. However, these vultures were not the avian kind—they were the A. Phagy kind, the formerly human kind, clawing and gnashing at the bloodied remains in the road.

As we drove by the herd of vultures, several of them looked up and reached towards the car while some could not be taken away from their meal.

As they reached their bloody hands in our direction I noticed that the tips of their fingers were torn apart with no evidence of finger nails and little of flesh. The bloody and bony stumps wiggled in our direction as Peter tried not to look at the vultures and slightly pressed on the gas a little harder.

Soon, we headed into a more thickly settled area of businesses. Peter told me we were heading through the heart of downtown. I felt a little uneasy about how thickly settled the population of undead may be as we passed through. Peter slowed down as we approached several cars abandoned in the road. We navigated between them like a suburban maze.

Eventually, we came to a complete makeshift roadblock of cars that had collided into one another. We stopped and looked for a way through. As we stopped, several undead slowly poured from the front doors of businesses and in between buildings. Quickly, Peter cut the wheel and drove onto a shallow curb. We drove half on the sidewalk and half on the town common. As we drove through, the car spat up mud and dirt as it tore apart the slightly overgrown grass like a bad lawnmower.

As the undead seemed to follow our car, we finally reached an intersection and got out of the common. We bounced the car back onto the road and quickly increased our MPH until the growing horde of undead faded away in the fog. "I hope that isn't a sign of things to come," I said.

"I wonder if I should kill the lights," Peter said.

"Do it."

Peter turned off the lights and it became slightly more difficult to see through the thickening fog. However, if we couldn't see, there was a great chance that the infected and decaying eyes of the undead wouldn't be able to see us very well either.

PETER

As we drove through the impenetrable fog, we passed several silhouetted bodies stumbling around. Without lights on, we simply came and went without them being able to tell what just passed them.

While we were driving, I considered telling Mike about the dream I had, but thinking about the state of him and his daughter made me just sit in silence as I did not want to put that idea into his head.

Soon enough, we turned onto the road of the grocery store and Mike began getting our things ready to go. The rain spat from the sky as thunder boomed in the distance.

Eventually, we pulled into the store parking lot, with a dozen cars parked in various spots. The store looked dark and made me wonder if somewhere along the line this area had lost power, which would make this one smelly trip. I pulled the car right near the store entrance and put it in park. Then, I took out the walkie-talkie and pressed the button. "Come in Fix-It," I said.

"Pete?" Jen asked on the other end.

"We've arrived at the store," I said.

"Any problems?" she asked.

"Lots of infected people downtown. Also, the weather seems to be picking up," I explained. "What about there?"

"We're all fine," she said. "Get in and get out."

"Copy that," I said as I looked into the dark store.

I put down the walkie-talkie and we grabbed a couple of flashlights that we had almost forgotten to throw in the car. The rain started to come down heavier and the thunder booms got louder as we picked up the pace and got our gear together.

"We'll each grab a cart," I said. "And we'll stick together."

Mike nodded as we stepped out of the car. As we each wielded a gun, shovel, and flashlight, we approached the doors only to find that they had been barricaded by dozens of shopping carts.

They wouldn't budge as we realized there could very well be people alive inside. However, after pushing the doors for a moment, we realized that the doors were not actually locked—only barricaded. Also, many of the shopping carts were covered in what appeared to be dried blood.

"What the hall happened?" I asked quietly.

"What do you want to do?"

"We should try to push our way through," I said to Mike.

Mike nodded as we set our gear down next to the doors. We then shined our flashlights into the store and looked around for a moment.

As we verified that nothing was moving in our general vicinity, we began pushing against the doors, slowly and barely budging the lineup of shopping carts.

Eventually, we pushed the door open a little more than a foot. I tossed the gear inside and squeezed through the opening. Mike quickly followed as I tried to pull the doors open further from the inside.

Once both inside, we examined the makeshift barricade and looked at the massive amount of dried blood covering several of the carts. After careful analysis, Mike brought up the idea that perhaps a number of workers—or whoever—locked themselves inside the store after one of their own had been bitten.

Then, perhaps, the infection spread within the confines of their hideout. After counting the number of cars in the lot, we figured that had to be at least thirteen people inside—possibly four or five times that number if the cars were full or if people without cars had attempted taking refuge there as well. And, if Mike's theory was correct, those thirteen could all be carrying the disease and ready to tear us apart.

The store was very dark and smelled terrible because of the rotting food and drink products. I wanted to puke at the thought of all the rotting meat, fruits, vegetables and dairy—especially the meat and dairy. The odors really reminded me of the horribly rotten burger I'd dreamt about. It made me queasy to think about, and smell, the decaying food.

While we took in the front end of the store, Mike suggested that we make some noise and draw out whoever may be hiding throughout the aisles and stockrooms.

I wasn't too keen on the idea of calling for these things, especially considering how many there could be lurking in the darkness. At the same time, I didn't want to run into them while looking for groceries.

As we explored the front of the store and considered Mike's call-out-the-beast(s) idea, three infected began stumbling towards us out of the aisles.

"Too late for my plan," Mike said in a frustrated manner.

We each put our guns down near a register and readied our shovels—more typical protocol. One of them spotted us in the dark; the other two were headed in our direction, but seemed more disoriented—almost as if they had just awoken with a bad hangover.

They moved slowly and we decided to do the same. I approached the one that spotted us. Mike stood back and shined the flashlight directly at the ghoul. I walked towards the illuminated infected from the side and in the dark. It stared at Mike, nearly salivating at the potential meal.

Then, as the creature's wrinkly lips curled around its teeth, I swung the shovel like a Louisville slugger and nearly hit a home run, crushing the skull of this fiend and sending his corpse to its final resting place. Immediately, Mike looked at the other two loiterers and found that they had seen us and were heading this way. Both of these two were sporting grocery store aprons and nametags.

One looked like a high school worker—probably a few years younger than me. The other was an older lady, maybe in her forties. As the youngster approached me, I read his nametag, Marc. I then realized that he was a bagger—a nice kid who had helped me the last time I was in here. He asked me about community college and if I thought he should go in a couple years.

As the decaying version of Marc approached me, I found myself saying, "I'm sorry" to him. Then, I proceeded with typical protocol as quickly and swiftly as possible. Marc's body fell to the ground and I turned away as Mike took the same action with the other worker — Linda.

Running into the familiar bagger boy really put a bad taste in my mouth. Mike could tell too as he began asking if I was okay. I grabbed my gear and a shopping cart and told him we should just make this quick. I didn't think about all the people I had become familiar with at this store and how I might run into several of them today.

MIKE

This was turning into a tough trip, tough and uncertain. Peter seemed quite bothered after dealing with the undead store employees upon our arrival here.

Aside from the corpses strewn about and some knocked over displays, the store looked like it hadn't been touched as far as looters went. However, another way to tell that some things hadn't been touched in a while was the terribly rotten smell — probably meat and dairy products that had likely been sitting out for days without any refrigeration.

We both headed towards the aisles with our gear and empty shopping carts. "Water is up here," Peter said hastily. We approached and found a decent amount of cases of bottled water. Then, we each loaded a few 24-packs into our carts.

We then heard some sounds emanating from the back of the store. "Shit," Peter said nervously. "Let's get the canned food and meds."

I nodded and followed him quickly a few aisles over to the soups section. We grabbed chili, baked beans, chicken noodle, clam chowder, creamed corn, baked potato, and creamy tomato.

After loading up, Peter said the medicine and pharmacy were at the back of the store—where we heard the suspicious noises. We readied our flashlights and shovels and headed back that way.

Meds were important, even just the simple over-the-counter pain relievers. We couldn't bear any of us getting sick and becoming a burden to the rest of the group right now.

So, we moved quickly and quietly towards the back. Peter led the way and did catch a glimpse of a couple infected several aisles away from the pharmacy. He seemed to intentionally look away and began to move faster. "Let's get it and go," he said impatiently.

As we made it to the pharmacy, we completely cleared out the shelves in front of the counter, tossing bottles of all sorts of O-T-C drugs into our nearly-full shopping carts. As we loaded the drugs into the carts, Peter insisted we go behind the counter and check for antibiotics. So, we did just that. At first, it seemed to be abandoned until we checked down one of the back aisles.

Standing there in a white lab coat with a reddish-brown dry stain of blood poured down the front was an undead pharmacist staring into the shelf motionlessly, almost as if the thing was looking for someone's medication. A moment after spotting the creature, it slowly turned to us as if it were waking from some kind of slumber. Its death stare fixated on us and I raised my shovel into the air. As I was about to swing at its head, Peter yelled, "Get back!"

I leaped back, thinking someone or something was near me. Then, the shelf that the former worker was staring at began to tip. Peter had pushed it over, knocking bags and containers of pills all over the place and trapping the undead against the wall. I quickly and blindly scooped up as many of the meds as I could and we both ran out of the section as the falling aisle created a loud crash and would surely attract the remaining undead.

We ran back to the carts and moved quickly away from the pharmacy as I thought of the irony of that worker suffering such a fate while being surrounded by life-saving drugs. Apparently, this virus or disease or whatever was far beyond the capabilities of pharmaceutical treatment.

As we rushed back, several undead were coming in our direc-tion—well over a dozen. Many seemed to come from the deli area, where it certainly smelled the worst. Some also seemed to come from aisles.

Peter quickly turned down one of the aisles in the middle of the store—the soda aisle. He ran into the aisle and ended up face-to-face with an undead stock boy. "Go around," he said as he rammed his cart into the stock boy, pressing him into the shelves. As the undead stock boy was trapped, I passed by swiftly.

Peter tried to pull his cart back and get away from him, but the stock boy reached relentlessly for Peter and simultaneously grabbed the cart. Peter then pulled the cart with all his force and sent the stock boy tumbling to the ground and the shopping cart rolling away from Peter. As Peter reached for the cart, and more importantly, his weapons, the stock boy began to stand—cutting Peter off.

"Shit!" Peter screamed as he backed away from the undead worker. Then, two more undead began coming down the other end of the aisle. Peter suddenly reached into his pocket and tossed the car keys to me. "I'm not leaving you Pete!" I shouted to him as

I grabbed the keys and shoved them in my pocket. He continued backing away as the stock boy reached for him. Quickly, Peter checked the other approaching undead and realized he didn't have much more room to back up.

Then, he quickly grabbed a twelve-pack of soda and smashed it directly into the stock boy's cranium, then proceeded to throw it down onto the ghoul, bursting several of the cans in the pack. At this point, the other undead were getting dangerously close to him, so I began heading over there with my gun in hand.

Peter ran in my direction and said, "Don't waste it!" as he continued running. We both grabbed our carts and took off towards the front of the store. We stopped by a wall, knowing we couldn't move the shopping cart barricade in time to escape the remaining undead—of which there were many. He pushed our carts to the side and went through a door marked: **EMPLOYEES ONLY**. The door was next to a large mirror that looked quite warped. The reason it was warped was because it was a two-sided mirror.

We entered the office and were relieved to discover that it was a small room and very easy to tell there were no stowaways. There was also a door leading outside where the workers could take a smoke break or something along those lines.

This was a prime exit for us, but we needed to get our shopping carts from outside the office. As we turned back to grab them, the two undead employees from the soda aisle were stumbling around in front of the double-sided mirror.

"Shit," I said quietly.

"I don't think they know where we are," Peter whispered to me.

"Maybe they'll keep moving along," I said.

One of them walked towards our shopping carts while the other walked up to the mirror. It stared directly at us without knowing it and let out a monotonous moan for a moment. We stood on the other side of the mirror staring at the creep. The creep still wore his uniform and the latex cleaning gloves he had on were covered in dry blood.

His face was dry and wrinkly with large bags under his eyes and a gash in his cheek. His blank stare seemed to penetrate the mirror as he continued his steady moan. I held up my gun as the sight of this thing began to send shivers up my shine. Something clicked and his stare intensified as if he heard us. His moan grew louder and his lips curled over his blood-stained teeth.

"Fuck it," I said firmly as I raised my gun.

Peter looked at me as I squeezed the trigger and shot the ghoulish fiend in the head. Peter covered his head and turned around as the two-sided mirror shattered all over the place. We looked at each other and then to the other undead who obviously heard us and were heading in our direction. Quickly, I swung the door open and Peter grabbed the carts.

He pulled them into the office and I quickly slammed the door. We then pulled them to the exit. As the undead stumbled to the broken window, we pressed our ears against the door and listened. We heard the sound of heavy rain and a steady rumble of thunder, but nothing else.

As the creature reached through the broken window, we realized he lacked the mental capacity to figure out how to climb through, but rather than waiting for him to figure it out, we slowly opened the door into the pouring rain and looked around. We saw no signs of anyone outside. So, we pushed our carts over to the car and started chaotically loading everything inside.

PETER

After a stressful mission, we finally got everything loaded up and hopped in the car, shielding us from the elements of Mother Nature and the undead. As we sat down in the calm atmosphere of the car's interior, I sighed in relief as Mike did the same.

"Let's not do that again," Mike said.

I nodded and put the key in the ignition. As we began to pull away, Mike noticed at least half-a-dozen infected climbing over themselves and the shopping carts, trying to exit the store. As I kept driving with the wipers on full blast, I figured it was a good time to radio the crew.

"Guys? Come in," I said.

"Pete? Or is that Mike?" Joey asked in return.

"Hey, Joey. It's Peter."

"Everything okay?" he asked.

"We're all right," I told him. "Heading back now. Let Jen know, okay?"

"Okay, man," he said. "I will."

"See you soon," I said as I put the walkie down.

We drove slowly through the stormy weather. As we came to the exit of the big lot, several undead started appearing in the fog. There were dozens scattered all over the place—more than any of us had seen at one time. We probably drew them out of hiding when we drove through before.

"Keep going," Mike said, sternly. "Just look for your openings and take them out. Don't stop!"

I nodded and kept driving through the hordes of undead lurking about and reaching for the car as we snuck through. They seemed to be a never ending mob of infected as we finally started to leave many behind us.

94

We kept driving through the storm of rain, fog, thunder, and undead. This time, we avoided downtown by taking side roads. The rain was treacherous at this point and would certainly not allow us to cut across the grass again without getting ourselves stuck.

Eventually, the hordes lessened and we only passed a few infected as we got closer to the hardware store. I let out a very small beep from the car as we pulled into the parking lot, just so they would know to let us in. We ran to the doors, leaving the food in the car for the time being.

Jen greeted us with some Fix-It Hardware t-shirts for us to change into and get out of our wet clothes. I handed the keys to Joey and explained to everyone that we would bring in the new supplies when the rain lessened a bit.

They agreed and all told us to relax. However, we then realized that we left our weaponry in the car—something that we didn't want to be without—especially with the amount of undead stumbling about the town.

Joey ran out to the car and retrieved the guns and shovels quickly as we explained to Tara and Jen what we had seen. They insisted we both take a break and try to get some rest. Jen then informed me that Sam had offered to sit by the window and keep a look out.

This would be her first time as she still had yet to get over Robbie's death. We both agreed that Jen would sit and watch with her to make sure everything would be all right.

I wasn't too thrilled about the timing of Sam finally showing some will power on the day that we discovered the mass amount of undead, but Jen would make sure everything was okay while Mike and I caught up on some rest after some of the closest calls yet.

LOSING IT

JEN

The rain finally started to let up as Mike and Peter were getting some rest. Joey and Tara brought in a couple boxes of canned goods from the car and began sorting through them by food and expiration date.

Sam and I sat by the front window and watched as they brought in the last boxes for the evening—waiting for daylight tomorrow to bring in the rest. They offered to switch with Sam and me after a while.

After they left, Sam looked at me for a moment with a blank look on her face. "Robbie's dead, you know," she bluntly said.

I looked away for a moment and slowly nodded. "I know, sweetie."

She just shook her head. "Whatever…"

Peter then walked out with the dog leash and got Fido ready to go outside. "I couldn't sleep," he said as he approached the door. As he was about to unlock the door, he turned to us and asked, "Has it been pretty quiet out there?"

"Yeah, we haven't heard anything but the wind," I added.

He nodded and headed outside with an anxious Fido. They walked around until Fido found a spot to go to the bathroom, right near Joey's back tire. As they were near the car, Peter was peaking inside, likely double checking all of the supplies from the store.

Then, Sam got up and started walking away from the window angrily and sat by the cash register. Suddenly, we heard a noise from outside. A voice. Two men were stumbling into the parking lot and one was badly wounded in the leg.

"Help!" the non-wounded one shouted. "Help us!"

96

Peter jumped back as Fido went crazy at the site of these strangers. "What the hell?" Peter screamed. Peter backed away quickly, tripped on the curb, and fell backwards.

They looked directly at us through the window as I leaped from my seat. "Guys!" I shouted. "Guys! Help! Come out here!"

As Peter fell on the ground, he dropped the leash and Fido's little frame charged towards the men with a bark fit for a pit bull.

"Shit!" Peter screamed.

"Oh no," I said as Joey and Tara ran out from the back room, followed by Mike.

"Fido!" Peter screamed frantically.

"Look!" I said, pointing out the window.

"Please!" the man shouted again.

Mike ran to the door and unlocked it, letting the two men in.

"Thank you. They were catching up to us!" he said

"What happened to your leg?" Mike asked anxiously.

Peter went to grab Fido, but he still seemed startled and ran into the dark road where we soon couldn't see him.

I ran to the door and stuck my head out. "Pete, come back!"

"Fido!" he shouted nervously again.

"Ugh," the wounded man said. "One of them, they… They bit me!"

Mike quickly grabbed the gun and pointed it at the wounded man. The other man then lunged at Mike and attempted to grab the gun.

"No!" the man shouted. "You're not killing my brother!"

Peter continued running back and forth around the lot and the road, "Fido! Fido!" he kept shouting over and over again.

In the commotion, Mike pulled the trigger, sending a shotgun blast in the store, luckily not hitting anyone. However, the shells pierced and completely shattered a portion of the front window. I saw Peter nearly fall to the ground due to shock. Then he ran back inside.

"Shit!" I screamed.

"What the hell happened?" Peter asked anxiously.

Mike violently pushed the man away. "Son-of-a-bitch!" he yelled.

During all of this, the wounded man had stopped moving and laid there still on the ground. His brother reached down and yelled, "Bobby? No!" as tears streamed down his face. However, as quickly as Bobby had passed, his body awoke and saw his brother as nothing but a fresh meal.

The undead Bobby lunged up and tore through his brother's neck. Joey ran towards them and pushed off the freshly bitten brother, then took some typical protocol to Bobby. Peter helped out and as the other brother quickly started to succumb to the infection, Peter did the same thing and took him out. As that threat quickly disappeared, the even bigger threat of a large open window started to sink into our situation.

PETER

All of this couldn't have happened at a worse time. We finally had a supply of food, water, gas, shelter - everything. Then, these two guys come from nowhere and all of a sudden we're out of a secure shelter with hordes of undead headed our way and a nice and messy cleanup needed in aisle one—not to mention, my mom's dog is missing in action.

Mike and I quickly pushed the fresh bodies out the door and locked it again—not that it mattered because of the gaping hole which used to be the front window. I quickly ran to the back room, looking for anything we could use to seal the window. Jen brought

Sam into the office. Jen was nervous about how Sam was feeling as well as her overall current state of mind.

Armed with their guns, Mike, Joey and Tara stood by the window, keeping a close watch on any potential threats. As I looked high and low for plywood or sheet metal or anything, I realized that all of the shelves holding back stock were made of metal beams and rods with long loose pieces of wood resting on them.

These were pretty strong and durable pieces as they were used to hold hundreds of pounds of tools and other merchandise. I grabbed some loose pieces and quickly brought them to the front window. But, we needed at least seven or eight more pieces and that would require emptying off the shelves—roughly an hour or two of work—an hour or two that we did not have at this point.

As I brought out what was readily available for the project, I told Mike where to find the nail guns, nails, and hammers. He quickly went to the aisle and ransacked everything that could be of use. Joey began to stage all of the wood as I brought it out and Mike gathered the needed tools. We had to be quick with this project as our vulnerability was through the roof—or broken window in this case.

Soon enough, Mike and Joey began to hammer in some wood on the bottom right corner. The window was tall, but as long as we covered the bottom, we would be all right for the time being as I'm fairly certain that these things could not figure out how to climb.

As they worked on preparing our shelter, I hastily emptied the shelves and retrieved more wood. I could feel each crash of the hammer in my heart as they were working and felt chills run down my spine as I thought about how many undead were loitering on the streets and hearing the clashing of the hammer as some kind of dinner bell.

I freed up two more shelves and quickly brought them out to Mike and Joey to cover as much space as possible. As I went through the swinging stock room doors, I noticed that the hammering had stopped. I figured it was good timing with me bringing the next pieces of board, but to my chagrin, I came through the swinging doors to see

Mike and Joey simply holding a board up and ducking beneath it with fear engraved on their faces as a handful of infected stumbled directly towards the store.

I dropped the extra shelves and dashed to the cashier's counter where I hid, not knowing what to do. They wouldn't have been able to get over the boards that we had already placed very easily, but our shelter was definitely not secure by any means.

I peeked around the counter and looked at Mike as beads of sweat streamed down his face. He looked at me for a moment, then at the gun lying on the floor next to him.

Quickly, I crawled across the floor, not knowing exactly where the undead were in relation to the window. Then, I grasped the gun and sat by Joey and Mike for a moment. As I stopped, Mike and Joey flinched as one of the infected seemed to be pushing against the wooden board.

We all looked up to see a pale bony hand reach over the wood and loosely clench the air repeatedly as if it were trying to grab onto something.

Suddenly, the pushing grew stronger and knocked the wood on top of us, allowing four infected ghouls to reach through the opening and nearly fall into the store.

I backed up and got to my feet and Mike and Joey sheltered themselves underneath the fallen board.

I stood up and aimed the gun at the ghouls. Their teeth gnashed together like rabid wolves and their lifeless eyes fixated on me in some kind of death trance. I cocked the gun and fired.

The shell tore through the two in the middle. Thick dark blood splashed on the boards and other undead individuals as the two permanently ended monsters fell to the ground. Mike and Joey quickly stood up and lifted the board above their heads.

"One, two," Mike said. "Three!" And they tossed the board at the remaining undead. It was a rushed decision, but it bought us some time as it sent them flying backwards into the lot.

"I'll get the other boards," I said as I frantically turned around to see Jen, Sam and Tara staring at the horrific scene. "It's all right," I said as Jen pointed to the lot. I turned around and saw well over a dozen infected stumbling into the lot.

"We can't hold it down," Mike said angrily as he grabbed the other gun.

Jen approached me quickly and asked, "What should we do?" as Fido ran into the lot and started barking uncontrollably, somewhat arousing the undead as they began barking in their own way right back at us and him.

"Get that dog out of there!" Mike shouted.

"Fido?" I exclaimed. "Fido! I've got to get him!"

Mike grabbed me and held me back for a moment. "Don't go out there," he said. "Look, they don't have any interest in him anyways."

I then looked outside to see the infected ghoul stumbling around the stressed Fido and was excited by the sounds of his barking, but Mike seemed to be right—they had no interest in harming or eating him.

A little relieved at Fido's situation, I then looked over to Joey and said, "Joey, go with Tara and clear a path to the back exit just in case."

Joey nodded and the couple ran to the back room to clear a path through the messy stock room.

Mike stood ready with his gun. "What do you want to do here, Pete?" he asked, as the undead got closer and closer to the store.

Suddenly, Samantha stepped forward and began walking to the window.

"Sam?" I asked curiously, then looked to Jen. "What's she doing?"

Jen stared outside. "Oh my…look!" she said.

I looked straight ahead and saw a familiar red Fix-It Hardware shirt walking towards us. As the figure got closer, it became clear that it was the corpse of Robbie. His long hair looked dry and crunchy and his face was covered in reddish brown dry blood and possibly dirt. He reached for us like any other infected soul would have.

I stood next to Sam and raised my gun. "Sam, get out of here, please."

She looked at me angrily. "Why don't you just shoot him, you asshole?" she said bluntly.

Not knowing what to say, I looked at her for a moment and lowered my gun.

"Do it!" she shouted at me.

Jen then approached us and put her hand on Sam's back. "Sam, why don't…"

"Shut the fuck up, Jen! It's Pete's fucking fault Robbie is like this in the first place!"

My breathing became heavy as I tried to hold back my frustration and anger. I tried to think of something—anything—to say in my defense, but all I got out was, "Jen, get her out of here, she's losing it!"

"She's already lost it," Mike said.

"Fuck off!" Sam said angrily and pushed me aside.

"Sam!"

She then ran to the window. "Robbie!"

"Sam! Don't!" Jen screamed.

Sam pulled off one of the boards and hopped over the bottom of the broken window.

"Sam!" Jen continued as tears streamed down her face.

Samantha then ran out into the small crowd of undead, exciting all of the infected to the point that they were almost roaring. She pushed several of them aside and ran to Robbie as if he were still alive and well.

"I'm sorry, Robbie," she said.

Robbie greeted her by wrapping his thin bony fingers around her arms. He leaned his head in and tore into Sam's neck with his gnashing teeth.

Jen lunged towards the window as Mike and I both grabbed her. "Samantha!" she screamed, violently crying at the brutal sight of our friend succumbing to this sickness.

As I wrapped my arms around Jen and pulled her to the back room, Mike fired his gun once more into the crowd of infected reaching through the window.

A few of them fell backward but were immediately replaced with others who stepped forward into the newly vacant spots lining the window.

"Fuck! We've got to move!" Mike yelled.

"Come on!" I said as I pulled Jen into the stock room.

Mike followed me as I glanced back at the window, only to see the dozens of undead piling on top of each other while trying to get to the window. The remaining pieces of glass along the trim broke off and stabbed the rabid infected as they reached through the window.

Soon, one began to hang through the window and it was only a matter of time before they started entering the store.

I turned away and ran into the back room. Jen viciously cried for the loss of Sam and ran into Tara's arms.

I explained that Sam was gone and we had to get out of the shop as fast as possible. Joey had created enough of a clearing to get to the back exit and we were ready to go.

Tara comforted Jen as best she could while Joey, Mike and I moved a large shelving unit in front of the swinging doors. We all agreed that even if we were taking off, we wanted to have something to slow down the infected.

After moving the unit in front of the doors, I took a look through the small plastic windows on the swinging doors and saw three undead getting to their feet after coming through the window—they were inside. Fix-It was now officially lost to the infection and Robbie had returned to his workplace, possibly where he will stay forever.

With no other options, we quickly took off through the back exit. Joey took out his keys and ran to the corner of the building. In the dark, he was able to see his car lit up by the lights of the store and we could all hear the continuous barking and growling of Fido.

As Joey was about to run over there, he noticed that the mass of undead was much larger than we had originally perceived and there was no way we'd be able to get Fido or get in the car safely— not without losing another member of our group.

I called Joey back and we made the tough decision to literally go on the run for the time being. I looked to the woods behind the hardware store and knew that they were thick and eventually led to the highway.

More likely than not, we would remain free of any contact with the infected in there. So, I told everyone that we had to stay close as the most dangerous aspect of this was how dark it was. We had to keep moving until dawn.

We began the run, moving at a steady pace away from the hardware store and into the unknown. I looked back as we ran, seeing the light of Fix-It—the only light in sight. I watched it for a moment until the brush of the forest began to grow thicker and the light faded into the distance.

Later, after hours of repetitious running through the thick woods, and several emotional stops, the trees started to space out more and the woods were finally coming to an end. The quiet highway came into view as the sky grew lighter and the sun began to rise.

Each of us basically collapsed into the grass hill that led onto the highway. We looked at one another and couldn't believe how far momentum had taken us.

The only problem now was that we were in the open, completely vulnerable and without any shelter or hardly any equipment.

DISPATCHED

DAVID

Our current base in Berlin, New Hampshire had just dispatched several crews of Military Police and Infantry Specialists on a mission for Operation Survival. My crew of eight had entered the field in two fully loaded Suburban Utility Vehicles and our current mission is to find any and all survivors in Massachusetts, focusing on our designated zones of one and three—Northern and Central.

Currently, we had been scouting a small town known as Hopkinton, where one of the first safe zones was established. The zone had officially succumbed to the Arthriphagy sickness, but the area was never combed for survivors.

We're also paying special attention to any homes or other small establishments that appear to be boarded up and/or sealed with survivors inside. Originally we were broadcasting via AM radio to these areas, but we have since ceased such efforts, as several rebel groups had used those broadcasts to find and ambush our rescue teams.

A lot of these groups had it ingrained in their minds that the government was behind all of this—something that's simply not true. This virus had spread globally in less than a week, wiping out entire countries and almost continents. So, we've done our best to stay off frequencies, only using a secure line for absolutely necessary intel between field crews and the safe zone bases.

I'm occupying the back of the SUV as the only Infantry specialist aboard. I'm with three M.P. officers, whom my Infantry buddies and I probably would've given a hard time in a different situation. But, these guys were all right. Officer Michael Sharpe is one of the Military Police I had been talking to a lot—he's about my age and was in the same training camp as me six years ago.

Officers Rickley and Heminez were also with us—they seemed all right, but they already knew one another from having been stationed together over the past few years, so they sat up front and didn't converse with us too much.

We sat in the back as we drove down a long highway—completely abandoned on our side and completely bumper-to-bumper on the other. With a few miles before we hit our next hot spot for suspected survivors, we were hitting higher speeds somewhere around fifty-five or sixty miles per hour.

Sharpe and I began discussing the events that we knew to be fact—the rapid outbreak of infection, the President and his cabinet retreating to an unknown and secure location, and the fact that the people infected with Arthriphagy were—for all intents and purposes—dead. Immediately, Heminez turned back to us. "What the fuck are you guys talking about?" he asked. "How can dead people get up and walk around? Hey, get a load of these guys Rickley!"

"Well," Sharpe said. "They don't sustain a body temperature, nor do they have a readable pulse."

"How do you know that?" Rickley asked.

"Well, I mean…"

"Ha! Yeah! What'd you do? Ask one of 'em to stay still while you checked the vitals or something?" Heminez said, cutting off Sharpe's answer.

"Whatever, man. Why don't you just keep your eyes on the road," I said.

Heminez glanced at the road, then back at us. "Ain't nothin' out there, man! Quit your backseat driving!"

As Heminez continued with his royally douche-like attitude, he completely ignored the other SUV in our convoy and the fact that it had stopped up ahead for something. Heminez smirked at us as he laughed and kept pushing down the gas pedal.

"Watch out man!" I shouted.

Rickley looked forward and smacked Heminez's arm. "Chet! Look out!" After hearing this from his partner in crime, he quickly looked forward and said, "Oh shit!" and slammed on the brakes and crashed into our partners' vehicle real hard.

Their SUV flew forward and crashed through the guard rail, flying down a grassy hill and eventually came to a stop at a tree. Ours followed them and slid to the side, smashing into the broken guard rail and almost rolling over entirely.

From this point, everything went dark until I came to moments later. I noticed that both airbags in the front had gone off, Heminez's door was pushed in, and the window had shattered because of the guard rail. I looked at him and Rickley—both did not move and if they were still breathing, it was so shallow that I could not detect it by watching any rising and falling action of their chests.

I looked over to Sharpe as he was slowly moving his head with his eyes still shut. Blood from his nose covered his face as he began to moan in a disoriented manner.

For a moment, I thought he was alive until I realized that he could be one of them. The stories we had been told were that you had to be bitten to become one, but I didn't fully believe that at this point. So, I grabbed my handgun and clenched it tightly as I watched the MP sway his head back-and-forth.

As his moaning continued, I became relatively certain that his body had been reanimated and he was now an Arthriphagy carrier. I held up my gun with the safety off and one in the chamber, ready to fire at the sight of his dead pupils. But to my relief, he finally opened his eyes and asked, clear as day, "What happened?"

"Thank God," I said. "I thought you were gone."

He looked at me for a moment, trying to piece together the situation, and then looked up at Heminez and Rickley's corpses. "Shit," he said. "Where's the other SUV?"

I pointed to the horrific sight out our side windows. "Right there."

Sharpe looked and saw the SUV smashed directly into the tree. From our vantage point, we discovered that the airbags had gone off and broken glass littered the scene. I quickly looked around and made sure the sound of the crash had not drawn any infected people to the area. After making sure that everything seemed all right, Sharpe and I slowly exited the vehicle and had planned on checking on the rest of our crew.

However, as we stepped out of the vehicle, I immediately got a strong smell of gasoline fumes. "You smell that?" I asked Sharpe.

He nodded and looked around the area of our vehicle where the guard rail had caused the most damage. "I don't see any signs of gas here," he said. "It must not be coming from our tank."

I nodded and cautiously proceeded to the other crash site. The gas could have been coming from the other SUV or from the highway, what with all the abandoned and crashed vehicles on the other side. However, as we got closer to their crash site, we found that the smell intensified quickly. I stopped for a moment and noticed smoke rising from the engine where the vehicle had crashed into the tree trunk.

"Move back!" I shouted as I ran back behind our vehicle. Sharpe quickly followed me as the SUV exploded with the rest of our crew inside. The explosion was massive and vibrated through my entire body as it pushed us onto the ground.

I began to crawl towards the highway to get away from our vehicle, just in case. Sharpe followed me after he got back to his feet. I looked back at the charred and burning remnants of the other SUV and couldn't help but think that I hoped they were already dead from the crash. And, while I wished we had gotten to them sooner, there was a chance that we'd be dead now too.

After a moment of staring at the wreck site, I took out my walkie-talkie and attempted to reach base for an extraction as Sharpe and I were officially on our own out here with no transport. However, the walkie-talkie seemed to have been damaged during the crash because all I got was static.

So, we tried Sharpe's as I was sure the MPs would have had the better equipment. To no avail, his was the same result as mine. We decided to give it a minute to be sure our vehicle wasn't about to go up in flames as well, then we would retrieve whatever useful gear we had inside and head out on foot in search of transport.

After retrieving some ammunition and our canteens, we headed out, taking a mile-or-so of the highway on foot. As we got a little further away from the crash site, I tried the walkie-talkie again, still to no avail. We were on our own for the time being and we both knew that could be quite a long time—especially if we couldn't find a mode of transportation. We both agreed that we would continue our mission and search for survivors while we looked for a way out for ourselves. After all, any survivors we might find could end up having a car that we could use to get back to Berlin.

As we came to a highway onramp that would lead us into town, we cautiously went in, keeping an eye out for survivors and infected people. We both knew from experience that the more thickly settled areas would harvest more infected. So, we moved quickly and quietly with our weapons ready.

Upon entering the town, we found many broken down and abandoned cars and trucks. However, many of them were without keys. If they did have keys, they were either totaled or left on in some way so that the tanks were empty or the batteries were dead. We kept moving down side streets and didn't see anyone—alive or otherwise, except completely dead corpses littered among the streets and sidewalks.

Just as we were about to give up, we came to an intersection where we looked a little further down the road and saw a couple of large signs hanging from the roof of a building. One was blocked by a tree, but the other said **SOS** in huge letters. Of course there was a chance these were put up a while ago and the people had come and gone or had left on their own accord. Regardless, we decided to check it out.

As we got closer, we noticed it was some kind of shop, a hardware shop. But, even if there were once people inside, there wasn't anymore. The entire place was crawling with infected hosts, lurking around the parking lot and on the inside.

There was a red convertible in the lot, but between the dozen stumbling around the lot, we decided not to risk our lives for something that wasn't even certain. After observing this mess for a moment, we both decided we should quietly get out of there before being spotted by one of those things. They weren't so bad if it was just a couple, but dozens gets more than overwhelming.

So, we continued on our way. After cutting across another smaller highway, we came to another thickly settled area. However, this place seemed to be more sprinkled with infected loiterers. We approached with extreme caution.

After passing several blocks, we came to an intriguing scene. There was a car that looked like it was used very recently. The skid marks leading up to its parking space were dark on the pavement and very fresh. To say you could smell the burnt rubber would be a bit of an exaggeration, but I didn't doubt that we only missed that sensation by a few minutes. Also, behind the car were two corpses that looked to have been bashed in the head with something, the pools of thick blood around them were definitely fresh and made us wonder if there were some survivors around.

The car was in front of a large brick factory building that looked otherwise void of people. After a moment of keeping ourselves hidden behind some trash cans on the other side of the street, a few of the infected came stumbling down the street. As Sharpe looked around for a few moments, he noticed something very strange. A man on the roof of the building, holding a gun and pointing it down to the ground.

We didn't know his intention; whether he wanted to take the infected out or if he was going to take us out. We also didn't want to take the chance that he took out the infected and then us by accident as I'm sure he hadn't seen many people with a heartbeat walking down these roads lately.

So after a moment of watching him watch us or the road or the infected, I decided it was time to make him aware of our presence. I readied my gun, aimed and fired—taking out one of the Arthriphagy carriers. As the creature's head exploded, it fell to the ground. Sharpe kept an eye on our mystery shooter as I took two more well-aimed shots, ridding us of the problem of the infected for the time being.

At this point, we had likely severely startled this shooter on the roof because as Sharpe watched him, he was frantically pointing his gun in all different directions. After a moment of realizing that this man was definitely no professional, I stepped out carefully, still holding my gun I. "Drop the gun!" I shouted to him.

I saw him look directly down at me and aim his weapon in my direction.

"I said put it down, sir!" I told him once more.

"Don't even think about it!" Sharpe chimed in. "We've got you and we don't mean any harm!"

From my vantage point, I could tell he was nervous and wasn't about to fire. So, I lowered my gun and told Sharpe to do the same. Reluctantly, he followed my orders and did so.

"Take it easy up there!" I said once more.

Then, out of nowhere, the large front doors to the factory clicked and creaked loudly as they began to open. Immediately, Sharpe and I raised our weapons once more when we noticed that the man on the roof had run away.

As I began to sweat, not knowing what we had walked into here, the doors opened all the way and a man stepped out slowly.

"Freeze!" I said, aiming my gun cautiously.

BACK ON OUR FEET

PETER

We were all exhausted as we sat on the side of the highway. The sun was rising and none of us had the energy to move—but we had to. We had to get back moving and find some kind of shelter. There were figures moving off in the distance and we had no immediate plan.

"What are…? Where are we going? What are we going to do?" an exhausted Mike asked.

Jen plopped onto the ground with dried teardrop streaks on her face. Her face was blank and she breathed heavily.

"We need to keep going," I said.

Tara crouched down next to Jen and rubbed her back as Joey looked up and down the stretch of highway with me. A handful of the undead were lurking about in each direction. They probably didn't know we were here yet, but it was only a matter of time. We observed the cars as well—scattered throughout the road, many with doors ajar and cracked up bumpers and sides.

"Should we try one of the cars?" I asked.

Joey looked around. "Seems like our best bet," I said.

"Lots of gas tanks are probably empty and I'll bet the batteries are long dead by now," Mike said. "I was in a similar situation to these people and I don't think I took the time to turn off my car when I had to take off."

"We might as well check out a few," I said.

Mike nodded and began walking onto the road and towards the nearest sedan. Joey and I followed, keeping a close eye on the lurking undead off in the distance.

As I began checking the idle vehicles, I noticed something moving inside a small sedan. Intrigued, and also a little nervous, I slowly approached the vehicle. At first, I thought it was a dog or something.

I peeked through the back windows and saw that it was a child that had been infected with the A. Phagy disease. He was buckled into the backseat and lacked the motor skills to unfasten the belt. I watched him for a moment as he slowly moved from side-to-side, trying to free himself from the safety harness that was now providing more safety than ever originally intended.

"Pete, you okay?" Mike asked.

"Yeah," I said as I quickly turned away from the disturbing sight of such a young person succumbing to this sickness. "I was just checking the car. You have any luck?"

"There's a pick-up over here that Joey found."

Mike and I quickly walked to Joey, who was standing next to a dark red pick-up truck. He was holding the front door open.

"Was that already open?" I asked.

"I just opened it," he said. "The keys are sitting in the ignition."

"Was it left on?" Mike asked.

"Not sure. We have to try it."

Joey then hopped into the driver's seat of the oversized gas guzzling truck. Mike and I stood at the door and watched nervously as Joey slowly turned the ignition key. The engine coughed for a long moment and then rumbled to life. We were hopefully home free — or *somewhere free.*

At the sound of the engine starting, Jen and Tara both stared up at us with hope. I could see Jen wipe her face with both hands. She was broken after the loss of Sam, but she knew there was limited time to mourn.

They began to pick themselves up as Joey leaned out the driver's side door and waved them over. There was no removing the smile on his face. Mine too.

Despite all the crap we had just gone through, we had caught a break; a working engine with a quarter of a tank of gas. Like I said, we were *somewhere free*.

JOEY

I was psyched to have found the pick-up. Despite it not being the most ideal or sporty vehicle, it would work just fine for what we needed—a way out.

We were officially back on our feet. Jen and Tara piled into the extra small backseat of the truck while Peter sat in the passenger seat and I got the nearly forgotten pleasure of driving. Mike hopped in the bed of the truck and had his gun ready.

So, we got the truck going and headed down the road—I think we were heading north or northeast. Cars and the infected were scattered all over as I slowly drove through, trying not to hit anything.

The truck wasn't in the best condition and we couldn't risk stranding ourselves again.

As we drove through the chaotic highway, the undead hosts perked up like starving animals at the first sight of prey. Their mouths hung wide open as their weak looking arms flailed in our direction.

When I looked in the rearview mirror I could see Mike holding up his gun. He was quickly moving the weapon left and right and I could feel his fear as we got dangerously close to each of the undead.

"Where are we going?" Tara asked.

"We're going to have to find somewhere," Peter said.

"What are we looking for?" I asked.

Peter simply shook his head. "I guess we'll know when we find it."

"Let's just get there," Jen said softly.

Peter nodded in agreement. "I guess we'll get off at the next exit."

"Sounds good."

As we continued through the still scene, which was once a fully functioning highway, we began to find cars clustered together more and more.

The exit was not far ahead on the right, but the paths between the cars seemed to bottleneck as we got closer. We could see the exit clearly and saw that no cars had been taking it as it was clear as day. However, getting onto the exit would be another story. The cars were either idle or had crashed all over the road, and it became questionable if we would have enough room to make it through.

Soon, we would have to come to a complete stop and survey the mess of cars and hopefully find a way through the wreckage. As we stopped, Mike shouted, "We've got to keep moving!"

Peter and I both looked back and saw that the dozens of infected people we'd passed were all headed our way. They were moving slow, but if they caught up to us, we would have to deal with more of them than we probably could.

"What should we do?" I asked.

Peter pointed to the last row of cars on the right. They were bumper-to-bumper—some literally touching bumpers—and very close to the metal guard rail. It seemed like our only route would eventually lead straight to the exit.

"Do you think we can fit?" Peter asked.

I shrugged and slowly pulled the truck in that direction. We were not going to fit. The opening was roughly a foot smaller than the width of the truck.

"No way," I said.

"Shit."

"Come on, guys!" Mike shouted from the back.

I looked around for a moment and saw no other opportunity. We could try to squeeze through, but if we became stuck, we could very well end up trapped, with no way out, waiting for the undead to snack on us.

"Just try it!" Mike shouted once more as the undead were getting closer and closer to the truck.

I looked back as I threw the transmission into reverse. Then, I backed the truck up ten or fifteen feet before I put it back into drive and slammed down on the gas pedal.

"Hold on!" I said.

The exhaust roared and smoked as we pushed the truck as hard as we could into the thin opening. Slamming into the small car in front of us, I was able to push it a few feet forward, creating enough room for us to squeeze into the little pathway.

With each side of the truck scraping up against the railing and the cars, we struggled as we slowly pushed forward. I could see Mike in the rearview mirror, struggling to hang onto the back of the cab as we jerked back-and-forth.

"Almost there!"

We kept pushing through as the horde of undead were now pouring into the small pathway now littered with side mirrors and shards of metal and paint.

"Keep going! Keep going!" Mike yelled.

We had about the length of four cars to go until the path would widen and we could get onto the exit ramp. Some of the cars were slightly further from the guard rail while others were rather close. This made for a constant struggle to make it through.

Soon enough, the cars widened the path and we eventually got the truck all the way through the little lane and onto the exit. The undead were hot on our trail as I sped up and flew around the exit ramp.

We were probably going around thirty miles per hour, but it felt as if we were on two wheels around the bend compared to the five miles per hour trail we had just gone through.

MIKE

We were finally off the highway and onto some side road. Judging by the contrast between the amount of cars here and on the highway, it became apparent that we were likely on some kind of evacuation route. It also became apparent that those evacuating didn't get very far.

After getting off the exit ramp, we soon passed the onramp and there were more bumper-to-bumper cars. I couldn't help but think of Ellie and how they might have been on one of these routes. I somehow kept the thought from driving me mad and kept my eyes peeled for any signs of safety or shelter.

We passed many buildings, but had no indication as to whether or not they would be suitable living arrangements. So, we kept driving for a while through the abandoned town, passing tipped cars, and gatherings of infected people.

Sometimes we came across roads that would have the remains of a serious car accident. Some were so bad that we were forced to turn around.

Suddenly, the car began to slow down. I looked ahead, expecting to see a horde of infected standing in our path or another multi-car collision. Instead there was nothing. There were a couple of cars scattered along the roadside and a large brick factory building next to us.

"What's happening?" I asked.

Joey quickly exited the truck and slammed the door behind him. "Out of gas," he said bluntly while shaking his head. Then, Peter also got out of the truck, followed by Jen and Tara.

"What now?" Tara asked.

Peter shook his head. "We're going to have to keep going. On foot I guess."

"What about this place?" Tara asked, looking at the large factory building.

I hopped out of the back of the truck and examined the building. It was old and the signs on the outside were worn. This place could have very easily been abandoned or shut down some time ago.

"Are we going to be able to hold this place down though?" Joey asked.

"Yeah, it is pretty big," Peter said.

"We'll never know unless we take a look inside," I said.

Peter nodded and looked up and down the road. "Let's give it a shot," he said as he approached the front entrance.

We all left the truck and went to the large factory doors at the front of the building. We approached cautiously and I kept my gun pointed at the doors. Peter grabbed the handle while Joey took the other gun. We both locked our sights on the questionable doors and waited as Peter slowly pulled the large doors.

Surprisingly, they opened. A small dust cloud puffed up as the heavy doors opened. Joey and I looked around as the daylight poured into the seemingly abandoned building. Slowly, I entered and looked around.

There was another large set of doors straight ahead with a chain and lock around the handles and a sign overhead that read "Hardhats and safety glasses required beyond this point." To the right of the large doors was a staircase, and to the left of the doors, were two rooms, likely bathrooms. They were marked with men and women symbols.

Peter walked through the small corridor and found a fuse box next to the locked doors. He opened it. "Lights, I think."

"Should we turn them on?"

"If there's anything in here, we might as well see them coming," he explained.

"Do it," I said.

He flipped a couple of switches and light poured through the cracks of the locked doors. "It works," he said as he continued flipping switches until the lights in the corridor came on, as did the lights leading up the stair case.

We proceeded to check the men's and women's rooms, which ended up being large locker rooms. They were empty, but there were things in the lockers—boots, hardhats, a couple of bags here and there.

This place wasn't abandoned after all, at least not originally abandoned.

PETER

After clearing the locker rooms, we were about to begin checking out the upstairs when we heard a pounding noise. It came from the other side of the locked doors. I placed my head on the door and listened for a moment. The pounding increased and it sounded as if there were multiple infected on the other side. I even felt the heavy doors shake as the pounding continued.

I looked back at Mike and he said, "Just leave it; they're not going to get through those doors."

I agreed and we began trekking up the ominous staircase. There were no sounds coming from any of the rooms. The stairs led to a long hallway with a few doors on each side; a couple of bathrooms, an office, a meeting room, and a break room. We checked out each room and found no signs of any recent activity—alive or otherwise. However, the meeting room had a large window that overlooked the factory—the work area behind those locked doors.

We looked and saw over a dozen undead stumbling around aimlessly. They had no idea we were here. But, they seemed a little confused, probably because of the lights.

The other rooms were pretty much what you'd expect. The office had nothing but a desk and a ton of paperwork. The bathrooms were bathrooms. The break room had a refrigerator with some soda, bottled water, and old lunches. Thankfully the fridge was still on; otherwise I didn't know how bad those sandwiches would have smelled. There were also a couple vending machines, a similar assortment to that of Fix-It.

We made the decision to make this our new living space for now. As long as the lock held on the doors to the factory, we would be fine, and I saw no possible way a couple of undead could get through that.

After making the decision to stay, Jen lay on the couch in the break room and got some sleep. Tara and Joey found some cards and magazines tucked away and started looking through them. Mike and I found another door which led to the roof. Mike decided he wanted to check things out.

So, he did just that and went up to the roof. Not long after he was up there, I heard shouting. It wasn't Mike. I couldn't tell who it was.

As I listened for a moment, I heard someone yell "Freeze!" I had no idea what was going on, but there was someone here for sure.

I ran to a window in the break room and saw something or someone crouching behind the truck. I couldn't make out who it was or how many were out there. I got up quickly and was going to run up to the roof when Joey stopped me and asked what was going on.

After I told him, he immediately grabbed the other gun and suggested we go down there. "Mike has the roof covered," he said. "We can catch them off guard from ground level."

It was a good idea. He and I quickly headed downstairs and stopped at the doors.

"Take it easy up there!" I heard from the unknown person outside.

I grasped the handle and looked at Joey. He nodded. "Open the door, I got your back."

So, I slowly opened the door. I stepped outside and a man pointed a gun directly at me. "Freeze!" he shouted.

I stopped in place as Joey stepped out and pointed his gun at the man. "Drop it," Joey said, sternly.

"We're not looking for a fight," the man said. "My name's Rich; we're United States National Guard."

As he spoke, another man stood up from behind the truck and raised his gun.

"Now please, put the guns down."

Joey and I looked at each other for a moment before Joey reluctantly placed his gun on the ground. The two soldiers quickly approached the building, still clasping their guns in their hands. We stood in place as they approached us and kicked Joey's gun out of reach.

"How many people you got in here?"

"Just a few," I said.

"Let's take a…"

Suddenly, the ground shook as a massive explosion knocked us off our feet. The boom echoed through the air. I couldn't believe this. After everything me and my friends had been through, to now die in an explosion, it just didn't seem fair. But sometimes, life isn't fair; sometimes it's just the way it is.

You can only do your best to survive.

The lights went out...

BONUS STORIES OF OTHER SURVIVORS

ANDREW HELMS

"The time is now 12:20 a.m. on June 15th, 2007. Nearly two days since the outbreak of the Arthriphagy virus. We will be going to the Channel Five Emergency Broadcasting System. Please stay tuned to your local A.M. Radio stations. Thank you. And, good luck to everyone."

That was it; we were done—possibly forever. I had been a news anchor for just a few years and something told me I'd just covered the biggest story ever. Most people in my position would've been thrilled to accomplish such a feat, but I just couldn't help but think that this was it. Not only the end of my career, but the end of everything.

By the time we went off the air, it was only me, the studio director, and an intern, remaining in the building. Most of the crew left on the 13th, after it hit the fan. They had families, friends and themselves to worry about.

Me, I just had some fish. I moved here from Michigan where my parents and sisters lived. I spoke with my mother when everything first broke out a couple of days ago. She assured me they were fine, but, the disease has since spread across the nation. There was no telling if they were okay.

Johnston, the director, was married to the job. I believe he had a wife at some point, but was now divorced. He was a tough guy. I think the gravity of the situation first sunk in when he gathered everyone in the studio on Friday and said, "There's no telling how bad things are going to get. If you're going to leave, do it now." About half the studio took off at that point. Within the next twenty-four hours, everyone else made their escape as well. I figured Johnston would've been annoyed, but he just got behind the teleprompter and started taking over all the behind-the-scenes work.

Around 3:30 in the morning yesterday, we all took a break and replayed the crucial video packages on a loop. Other than the three of us, everyone else had left. Johnston approached Julia and I and said, "Just go if you're going to."

Julia was an eager young woman whom neither of us knew much about. She was straight out of school and mostly covered stories for the website, but had recently been spending more and more time in the studio.

She reminded me of myself when I broke into the business. I respected her. Johnston had put her on camera duty after giving her a brief lesson.

"I'm staying," she said.

"Me too."

We were there for the duration. After taking a break for a few hours and getting some sleep, I awoke to the smell of coffee filling the studio. Johnston had the brew going and it almost felt like everything was normal.

The smell of freshly roasted beans filled the studio as it did every morning. We all met in the studio and Johnston informed us of a new batch of stories we would air throughout the day.

Apparently, the President would be addressing the Nation later. These were the moments that made me realize we were covering something big. So, we did just that and worked rather smoothly together.

I think work became a vice for us. We didn't have to deal with the terrors going on in the real world. We were simply reporting it and that casual work feeling we often got while reporting the news made us a little numb to the true severity of the situation.

Eventually, the President's speech came on via satellite…

"My fellow Americans, today, the thirteenth of June, is a day that will live in infamy. The United States of America has seemingly been overrun with a virus that has been labeled 'The Arthriphagy Virus.' This is containable and without a doubt, curable. I ask those out there to seek refuge somewhere safe and secure, especially those on the West coast. Where there is little sign of infection, for safety sake, please relocate yourselves to a local safe zone. Those on the East coast, outside of a safe zone, please stay where you are, and signs on the rooftops are helpful to our search teams. Listen for helicopters. We have teams all over the country, as well as the best doctors in the world developing a cure as we speak. In no less than seventy-two hours we will have this situation entirely under control. Remain at your current location until our search and rescue units locate you. This is an obstacle like no other. We will overcome this. America will overcome. Mankind will overcome. May God be with us through these trying days."

That was one of the last things we reported. The President had done his best to assure the people that everything would be okay, but the tone of his voice and the look on his face suggested otherwise. After the speech, Johnston got word that we would be switching to the emergency broadcasting system. We were off the air.

After finishing the final broadcast, I sat at the desk, staring at the camera. I did so until Julia asked me, "Mr. Helms, are you okay?"

I didn't respond until she asked me again. Then, I said, "It's Andrew. Please call me Andrew." She was always very punctual and aware of maintaining a professional attitude, but I felt that we had been through something more than your typical workday. In my opinion, we were on a first name basis now. After a moment of both of us remaining in our positions, Johnston came into the studio and looked at each of us.

Without saying a word, he just looked around the studio. He'd lost the ability to do his job and I believe he really didn't know anything else at this point in his life.

"You're both free to leave," he said to us.

"What are you going to do?" I asked.

He shook his head and walked slowly through the studio and into his office. He closed the door behind him. Julia stared at the door for a moment and then gazed back to me. "Is he all right?"

"How could he be?" I asked in response.

She nodded. "Are you going to leave?"

"Not sure. This is the longest shift I've ever worked." I didn't know what we were going to do. We really had no idea what it was like out there. Of course we'd received reports, but considering we were arguably the most informed people in the world, we had maintained a serious ignorance about the world around us.

Yes, we knew how to deal with coming in contact with infected people. Yes, we knew the signs, symptoms and causes of infection, but what it was like coming across an infected person was something we had yet to see.

It made me wonder if we should even attempt to leave. So many people have succumbed to infection. We had gone the entire time without having to worry about our safety.

This place was locked down and other than eventually running out of resources to live, we were completely safe from infection.

As I was thinking about this, I looked up and noticed Julia — she was crying. She tried to hide this fact, but it was evident. I got up and walked over to her. "Are you okay?"

She nodded and wiped her face. "I've dreamt of being involved in events like this, but now… Now, I just don't know how I feel."

She was a spitting image of me. I crossed all sorts of professional boundaries and hugged her. She hugged me back and really broke down. "I'm sorry," she said. "I just feel like none of it matters anymore. We're done and now we're just stuck here."

"It matters," I said.

She wiped her face again and stared at me, awaiting an explanation.

"We stayed," I said. "We stayed and we helped anyone watching by giving them the necessary information they would need to survive. Everyone who left, they were the ones who didn't matter in the end. You and me and Johnston, we stuck it out. It's because of us that tons of people will make it through this."

She let out a small smile.

"If it were up to me," I said. "I would definitely give you a promotion."

She laughed. "Thanks… Andrew."

I nodded and looked to Johnston's door. After a moment, we both decided to go see if he was all right. I knocked on his door — something no one ever did. If Johnston was in his office with his door closed, you would simply have to wait.

He didn't answer, but something told me it was okay to enter. I slowly turned the knob and peeked inside. He sat at his desk, typing something relentlessly. As I entered the office with Julia behind me, he didn't acknowledge us.

"Johnston," I said.

He continued to type for a moment. Then he stopped and stared at his computer screen and printed out whatever it was he was typing.

"Johnston," I said once more.

He looked at me as he pulled the document from the printer. "Is everything all right?" he asked as he looked at the paper and folded it up and put it in his coat pocket.

"What did you write?"

"The website's last article. Channel Five has signed off."

"What are you going to do now?"

He shook his head. "I don't know."

I he three of us went to the conference room and sat around the large table in the middle of the room. We each poured a cup of coffee and sat in silence. The television had the CHANNEL 5 EMERGENCY SYSTEM logo plastered on the screen. The words STAY TUNED FOR UPDATES scrolled along the bottom.

After a moment, Johnston got up and turned off the TV. He stared at the blank screen and looked at his watch. "Time of death: 3:25 a.m."

I stared at my coffee, not knowing what to do or say. Julia was concentrating on her cell phone, then put it on the table. "Time of death: 3:25," she said.

Johnston and I looked at her.

"My phone," she said. "I've been using it sparingly. My charger is at home. The battery is finally dead. I don't know if I'll ever charge it again."

Johnston sat back down at the table, this time closer to us than before. "Thank you both for all that you've done," he said.

"Thank you," Julia said.

"It's been a pleasure," I added.

Johnston nodded. "I suppose we should decide what we're going to do."

"Should we sleep?" Julia asked.

"That's not a bad idea," I said. "If we're going to leave, we might as well wait for the sun to come up."

"Get some rest," Johnston smiled. "We'll figure things out in a few hours."

I awoke on a couch in my office several hours later. Julia was curled up in a chair, as she didn't have an office of her own, though she probably had several to choose from at this point. But I got the feeling she just didn't want to be alone.

I rose and looked out my window. The sun was up and weather-wise, it seemed like it would be a nice day.

Suddenly, there was a knock at my door—it was Johnston.

"I figure we have two choices," he said. "We can get some signs on the roof to let rescue teams know we're here, or we can get out of here and make our way to one of the safe zones."

"We do have an approved list of them, right?" I asked.

"That's right, and I haven't heard any air traffic since yesterday."

"What do you think we should do?" I asked.

"I think...I think we should get the hell out of here."

"Me too," Julia agreed. She'd been awake without us knowing.

I looked at both of them and nodded my head slowly. "Let's do it then."

We gathered some things together and decided we would head out to the safe zone in Warren, Massachusetts. The list was up-to-date from eighteen hours ago, so hopefully nothing had changed. After I felt ready to go, I went and sat at the broadcasting booth. I shuffled through the papers leftover from the broadcast and looked at the camera for a moment. "This is Andrew Helms at Channel Five News signing off," I said to the studio.

Julia walked into the studio. "Great job."

I smiled at her. "Where's Johnston?"

She pointed to his office. The door was closed again.

"What about you? Are you ready to go?" I asked.

"I don't think I'm coming with you to Warren."

I stared at her, not knowing what to say. Was she serious? What was she going to do? Abandon us after all we'd been through?

"I have a family, a boyfriend," she explained. "I need to see if they're…I just need to see. After that, I'll come to Warren."

I nodded as Johnston came out of his office. Julia once again explained her situation to him. "I hope you find them," he said.

"Thanks," she called as we exited the studio.

On our way out, I looked around one last time and thought about how this place had become my second home. How much I'd grown as a person and defined my life as a news anchor.

It was surreal to think that I might never step foot in the studio again. Johnston seemed to know what I was thinking, and he gave me a reassuring nod and patted me on the back.

We finally left the studio and walked down the empty halls of the typically buzzing building. As we made our way through, Johnston explained that he and I would take a news truck as its doors were solid and the equipment might come in handy.

"Are you sure you don't want to come with us?" I asked Julia when she followed us to the parking garage.

"I need to go see, and I can't ask you to come."

"It's all right," Johnston said. "We'll see each other soon."

The garage was under the building and gated off from public access. We looked around thoroughly, as we couldn't be too careful. The garage was empty other than our own cars and several news vans. Julia was parked far away, so we drove her to her car, then we each drove out of the garage. The gates opened as Johnston swiped his card. This simple thing made me think about how things used to be.

I wondered if things would be fixed or if the power would eventually go out and we would perhaps be the last people to activate these electronic locks.

Julia pulled out behind us. She beeped twice as she turned right and we went left. Johnston beeped back and we began our journey.

As we rode through town, we saw no signs of people anywhere—infected or otherwise. We drove by several cars. Some were crashed, some parked, and some just abandoned.

I entered the address the list provided us with for Warren, Mass into the GPS. It was on Main Street—likely the Town Hall or something similar. According to the GPS, we would be there in a little less than an hour. We expected some detours though.

"Thanks again for sticking it out back there," Johnston said.

"I didn't know what else to do."

He nodded and shrugged.

"What was your last article about?" I asked.

He simply patted his chest pocket. "Someday."

I was curious, but didn't want to pry, so I dropped the subject. We took a turn as the GPS dictated and saw a group of people ahead—infected people by the looks of them. They looked like they were tearing something apart in the middle of the road.

"What the hell is this?" Johnston asked.

"This," I said, "is what we spent the last couple of days reporting on."

He shook his head in disgust.

I couldn't believe it either. We were finally being exposed to reality without the buffer of our familiar workplace. We both sat and watched for a moment in the idle van.

Then Johnston switched the gear back into drive and started moving forward. He slowly drove past the horrific sight and we didn't say anything more about it.

As we passed them, I looked in the side mirror and watched when some of the infected reached for our vehicle.

Their fronts were covered in what appeared to be blood. I don't know if Johnston noticed, but I didn't tell him.

As we continued on our way to Warren, the image of one infected individual stuck with me. He almost didn't look human anymore.

He had light brown hair and his face was covered in what looked to be a mixture of dirt and dried blood. His eyes looked dead when they stared directly at me, and his lips, they were gone. I saw all of his blood-stained teeth as he gnashed them in my direction.

"You okay?" Johnston asked.

I nodded and stared out the window. He knew something was up. I just couldn't get the image out of my head. That creature—that *thing*, it used to be like me. It used to be human, but it just wasn't anymore.

This sickness was even worse than I could have ever imagined, despite having seen footage and reported information on the details of it.

I thought back to when I was first told what was happening. They took me aside after we'd filmed the morning news.

"Something's happening," Barbara, one of the assistant producers told me. "A disease has broken out in New England."

"Like a form of the flu?" I'd asked.

"No, this is different" she'd said. "We're going live and exclusively covering this."

"Is this big?" I'd asked. If we were going live, it had to be big.

"Looks like it," she'd said bluntly.

Looking back, I felt sick to my stomach at how selfish I was. I was damn near excited at the fact that I was going to get to cover an emergency broadcast.

Some anchors live their entire lives without ever getting an opportunity like that, and it was beginning to seem like there wasn't much of my life left to live.

I kept thinking that Johnston would turn a corner and come across some military trucks or a makeshift base or something. But we just kept going, passing infected people, abandoned cars, accident sites and other unreal scenery. We hardly spoke; we had no idea what to say.

Nothing seemed right. We couldn't speak about what was happening as any words we would try to form would just fall short. I wanted to pinch myself — there was no way this was real. I thought about the little things.

I thought about how I'd been planning on cleaning my fish tanks this weekend. I thought about the Red Sox tickets I had for the June 25th game against the Orioles.

I even thought about how my credit card bills were due in a couple of days. The mundane things began to haunt me and I was sure I would never get the chance to complete any of those tasks.

I kept thinking about my fish. It had only been a few days and they were probably all doing absolutely fine. Other than being a little hungrier than usual, they were probably swimming around without giving any thought to the current state of things. I envied them.

That's right, me, a successful news anchor, was envious of a dozen African Cichlids. I smirked at the outlandish—yet true—idea.

Soon, we had left the city behind and we found ourselves on a quiet road. It seemed quite clear as we looked as far as we could see in all directions. There were a few cars on the shoulder, but for the most part, it looked like it might just end up being smooth sailing for a little while.

The GPS began barking orders and we went straight for six more miles. Six miles on this clear road? Perhaps our luck was turning around. Johnston began stepping on the gas and for the first time during the trip, he exceeded the speed limit. Instead of crawling through mazes of traffic and debris, we were now hitting 55-60 mph!

We were cruising; passing small businesses and a couple of infected people here and there, but nothing like what we'd seen previously.

But then something big happened. A man darted out into the road, a seemingly healthy man. He was running from an infected person. He ran right in our path. Johnston slammed on the brakes and swerved away from him, but when he almost struck the infected person, he lost complete control of the vehicle.

The van swerved around as he tried to regain control of the steering wheel.

"Shit!" he cried.

"Keep it steady!"

He kept swerving, the van coming up on two wheels. Then, suddenly, we crashed.

I opened my eyes and looked at the ground for a moment as I tried to find my equilibrium. After a moment, I realized that the van had flipped over. I couldn't tell what we'd hit, but we were down for the count.

"Johnston…" I muttered. "You all right?"

I looked over to him, and saw that something had smashed right through his window and basically crushed his head. I reached over and checked his pulse. I knew what the result would be, but I had to check anyways. He was gone. I sat there and looked at him, the man who used to be my boss, a man I grew to look up to.

He was dead and I couldn't help but think that he might have been the last person I would ever speak to. I wondered if Julia was doing okay. I hoped she'd found her family. I hoped she was doing better than me.

I looked around the van glad to be alive. My side of the van was lying on the pavement with the windows shattered and the windshield smashed up against a telephone pole. I figured it must have flipped and slid on one side until it hit the pole. I was very lucky to be alive, but very unlucky to be where I was. I didn't see an easy way out of the wreckage. Then I saw that I might be able to climb out of Johnston's window.

I decided to get moving. I went to unclick my seat belt but it was stuck. The button would not press down. I began to shake in panic. I pulled on the belt, hoping somehow it would open. No luck.

It wasn't budging. I began searching for shards of glass large enough to cut through the belts. The pieces were pretty small and were from safety glass but I still had to try. I found one that showed some promise, but only ended up cutting up my hand rather than the belt.

I wanted to cry but nothing came out. Everything had happened so quickly. I looked at Johnston's corpse and thought about the past few days.

I thought about Julia. I thought about the broadcasts and the words 'stay where you are.' Perhaps I should never have left the studio. There, I'd been as safe as my African Cichlids.

After thinking about the studio, I remembered Johnston's last article on the website. I looked at his body and his chest pocket. It was within my reach.

I felt as though I should read it. Work was his life and I needed to read his last act. Somewhat reluctantly, I reached into his chest pocket and pulled out a folded-up piece of paper, slightly stained with his blood.

I unfolded it and began to read:

My name is Johnston Hall. I'm the producer here at Channel Five News. It's been an honor to report to you the news of this outbreak.

Arthriphagy is something we may never understand or conquer. This is a new chapter in the history of humankind. I hope we will prevail and carry on. I hope that people like Andrew Helms and Julia Blackfield will lead us into the days of tomorrow.

During these last few days, we've stuck it out until the end. I believe we won't survive this. We've informed any survivors out there with lifesaving information. This has been my goal in life. I've helped bring the most important news ever to the public's attention.

Perhaps this was my purpose. If so, I'm glad that I've had the privilege to help in saving some lives.

I can only hope Andrew and Julia feel the same way. Thank you both. And to anyone reading this, thank you. I wish you all the best of luck in this trying time.

This is Johnston Hall for Channel Five News. Signing off.

I stared at the words on the page. They were powerful. I felt his voice in them. I slowly folded the paper back up and put it in his chest pocket.

"Thanks, Johnston."

Then I heard some kind of scratching noise. I looked up and saw an infected man trying to reach through the broken windshield.

He was staring right at me with those dead eyes. I was still trapped in my seatbelt, there was no way for me to escape. I looked at him for a moment, then closed my eyes. I waited for the end.

MARC

"It's for you, Marc! Phone! Marc, get the phone!"

"Okay Mom, I got it, you can hang up now! Hello?"

"Hey, Marc, it's Rich Jacobs from the store."

"Oh, hi Rich," I said. Rich was the manager of the deli at the supermarket I worked at. I was immediately very curious why he was calling me.

"Sorry to bother you. I know it's Friday and you probably have plans, but would you mind coming in today? You can work the full day for time-and-a-half."

"Oh! Uh, yeah sure," I said. "I can be there in an hour."

"Thanks so much," he sighed in relief. "Everyone called out and we really need some help!"

"No problem. See you soon."

As I hung up the phone, I nearly did a flip with excitement. I'm going to community college in the Fall and need all the money I can get. I was looking at a solid eleven hours of time-and-a-half today! I quickly calculated it out and saw I'd be getting roughly a hundred and forty dollars. It would all go straight to the bank!

I got ready for work. My mother had the day off, but had been watching TV all day. While I was grabbing a glass of milk before leaving, she barged into the kitchen and screamed, "Where the hell are you going?"

My mother could definitely be tough to deal with at times, but this caught me off guard. "What?" I said as I turned to face her.

"Are you going to work?"

"Yes? Why?"

"Have you seen the news at all?"

Even more confused than before, I tilted my head and asked once more, "Why?"

"There's a bad flu going around!"

I couldn't help but smirk and think of all the recent diseases that we were supposed to be scared of, like the avian flu, EEE, West Nile, SARS, bubonic; the list went on and on.

Sure, I understand that these did claim lives and were a big deal for some people. But unless you're very young, very old, or immune compromised, it most likely wasn't going to be a threat to you. I didn't qualify for any of those prerequisites.

"I think I'll be all right, Mom."

She shook her head with disapproval. "Don't you bring that flu back here!"

I nodded as I took my keys off the hook on the wall.

She retreated back to the living room and simply said, "Bye."

I waved and left for work.

I hopped on my bike and while riding, I noticed a severe lack of people. Cars drove by sporadically and much faster than usual.

I had about three blocks to ride before I'd reach the store and I saw absolutely no one outside other than those cars.

When I reached the store, there were about fifteen cars in the parking lot. It looked like an incredibly slow day.

I was greeted immediately by Rich when I entered the store. "Oh good, you're here!" he said, "Go punch in and start unloading the pallets for me."

"Okay," I said as I quickly headed to the back room.

"Pay attention to the speakers, too. I may need you to come help ring people out. If so, I'll page you to the front."

I nodded and continued on my way.

Hours later, I had unloaded most of the stock. There were only a few customers in the store. One wasn't looking too good. He was looking for the Pharmacy, only no one had shown up for that section, so Rich had to assist him with finding the most efficient over-the-counter stuff. I felt bad for the man—he really didn't look too good.

His leg was all bandaged up and he was complaining that the hospital had turned him away. Rich and I talked about it after we helped him out. Rich said it looked like he had a bad infection—not the flu.

Rich still seemed weary of the shopper, as did I. So, after our talk, he decided to go inform Linda—the cashier. She was a middle-aged woman, very nice and mother-like.

She had trained me during my first week and was constantly telling me things like, "You're such a nice boy, don't go off to college and become a drinker now."

I explained to her that it was just community college and I'd still be here part time while still living at home. But, she still seemed concerned that I'd adopt that lifestyle. And, to be honest, I wished I could. I wished I was going away to school, but we didn't have enough money for that.

We didn't have enough money for this school either—hence the reason I was working my ass off at this job all summer, and the reason I was one of the only people to show up during this possible pandemic scare.

As I stood there in the soda aisle, pondering over my life choices and for some reason Linda's opinion of them, Rich's voice came over the loud speaker and said, "MARC TO AISLE TEN FOR ASSISTANCE PLEASE! MARC!"

I quickly put down the boxes of soda and sprinted down the empty aisle. A couple of aisles over, I found Rich, standing over the sick man. He'd collapsed to the floor.

"Go to the register and have Linda call 9-1-1," he said to me very bluntly.

"Is he okay?" I asked.

"How should I know? Get going," he said.

I quickly ran through the store, calling Linda's name. I came around the corner and found her standing at the register, reading a magazine.

"Linda!"

She looked up. "What's wrong?"

"Call 9-1-1, a customer's sick."

She immediately picked up the phone. "Is it the flu that's going around?"

"I don't think so," I replied. "He has some kind of wound on his leg. Maybe it's infected."

She reached under the register and pulled out a white box—a first aid kit, and handed it to me.

"Take this, I'll call."

I grabbed it from her as she began dialing.

I ran back to aisle ten and was shocked to find the man walking in my direction.

"Sir, are you okay?" I asked. When I looked past him I saw Rich sitting against the shelves grasping his arm, which was bleeding profusely.

"Rich?" I said curiously.

"Get away from him!" Rich yelled. "He's crazy!"

"But Linda gave me the first aid kit," I said, completely oblivious to what was happening..

Rich began getting to his feet as the man kept stumbling in my direction.

"Toss the kit," Rich said, "Over here, then get away from him."

I did as he said and threw the kit. It landed on the floor and the man turned back towards Rich when he heard the sound of the kit crashing against the linoleum. Rich grabbed the kit and started sprinting down the aisle away from the sick man.

I didn't know what to do, so I ran back to the front of the store and found Linda at the register. She was holding the phone and listening. Then she slammed the phone down on the counter and shook her head.

"What happened?" I asked.

"No answer," she said, "No...answer..."

"What do you mean?"

"There was no answer," she said adamantly.

"On 9-1-1?"

She nodded and covered her face with her hand.

After a moment, Rich came stumbling around the last aisle, holding the first aid kit and still bleeding pretty badly.

"Oh my God, what happened?" Linda asked.

Rich shook his head and stopped at the register. He plopped the kit down on the counter and held his arm for a moment while shaking his head.

"Are you okay?" I asked.

He continued to shake his head and said, "That guy... He bit my damn arm."

"What?!"

"I went to check his pulse. I couldn't find one..." he said, "Then... then he just...I don't know, he grabbed onto me and bit my friggin' arm."

"Oh my God," Linda said again, covering her mouth.

Rich opened the kit and asked, "Did you call 9-1-1?"

She nodded.

He stared at us as he waited for a follow-up to what happened when she called.

"They didn't answer," I said.

He gave me the same look I'd given Linda.

He wrapped up his arm while Linda tried 9-1-1 once more. After a moment, Linda once again hung up the phone and shook her head. Rich kept pressure on his arm and started walking away from the register.

"I'm not feeling so hot," he said. "I'm gonna, uh, go sit over here for a bit."

Linda and I looked at each other worriedly for a moment as Rich stumbled over to a line of wooden benches set up along the wall.

We both looked up when the sick customer came fumbling around the last aisle. He was moaning and basically walking on one leg while dragging the other behind him.

"Oh my word," Linda said.

"Rich," I said, "What should we do?" As I looked to him for an answer, he seemed dizzy as he began tilting his head back and closing his eyes.

I looked to the man and said, "Sir, please take it easy." He didn't acknowledge me. Rather, he kept coming in our direction.

"Sir!" I called out again. "Please calm down. Have a seat." Again, it was to no avail, he kept walking our way. Linda stepped out from the register and approached the man.

"Okay sir," she said calmly. "Please come over here and sit down. Help is on the way."

She walked right up to him and reached out to grab his arm and assist him over to the benches. As she reached out, he intercepted her and grabbed her arm, then lunged at her, making a sound I can only describe as a muted roar. He sank his teeth into her arm.

"Linda!" I called out as she screamed in shock.

She fell back and the man landed on top of her.

"Oh my God!" she yelled. "Get him off me!"

I looked to Rich and saw that he was still out of it, so I grabbed a Hostess display stand by the register and approached the customer, whacking him over the head with it.

He didn't acknowledge me, so I took the bottom of the stand and pushed it into his side, rolling him off Linda. She lay on the floor, crying as the man struggled to get to his feet.

I reached out my hand to help Linda up, but she refused.

At this point, the man was up and he looked directly at me. He slowly began to approach me, nearly stepping on Linda in the process. I grasped the snack display tightly and backed away from him.

He reached out his arms and came towards me. I swung the snack stand and hit him in the face. He fell backwards and tripped over Linda. I pulled her out from under him as he rolled around on the floor.

"Are you okay?" I asked her.

She grabbed onto my hand and just looked at me. Suddenly, her grip grew tighter as the man bit into her ankle.

"Oh God!" she screamed once more.

"Damn it," I said. I let go of her hand and rushed to the register. I didn't know what I was doing, but I grabbed the monitor. I unplugged it and picked it up, the wires hanging beneath it like muscles and tendons from a decapitated head. Holding the monitor, I looked down at the man gnawing on poor Linda's leg, closed my eyes, and brought the screen down on him.

The screen smashed over his skull and his body suddenly went limp. I opened my eyes and tears began to well up as I looked at his lifeless carcass. I'd just killed a man! Linda's breathing had slowed noticeably as her gushing blood created a pool around her.

Though in shock myself from what I'd done, I mentally realized Linda might have had an artery or important vein severed when the man bit her.

"Rich, we need to get her some help," I said as I looked over to him. He was gone. I had no idea where but he was not on the bench anymore. I noticed a trail of blood leading away.

"Rich?" I called, looking around the store front.

Then I heard something—a mumble or moan or some kind. At this point, I turned around and saw him; Rich, standing a few feet away from me with a blank expression on his face—similar to that of the now dead customer.

"Rich, please, we need to get you some help," I said desperately.

He grunted back at me as he threw up his arms and made his way toward me. This time, I decided to run and dashed for the doors.

He came after me slowly but steadily. I continued trying to reason with him, but it didn't seem like he was aware of his surroundings. He just wanted to get to me for some reason.

I got to the doors and looked outside to see that night had fallen. The parking lot lights illuminated a number of people off in the distance. I couldn't go out there, for all I knew, they were freaking out just like Rich and the customer. I watched for a moment, forgetting about Rich coming up behind me. Suddenly, he roared and lunged at me, wrapping his arms around my body and sinking his teeth into my shoulder.

I screamed as the flesh was torn from my body, and my shoulder felt warm as blood seeped into my shirt.

I spun around, throwing him into the glass doors. His bite released and I backed away from him.

My blood dripped from his rabid-looking mouth and he gnashed his teeth in my direction. It was disgusting; something was definitely wrong with him.

I kept backing up until I reached a line of shopping carts along the wall. I grabbed one and ran it towards him—sandwiching him between the cart and the doors.

As he stumbled backwards and outside through the door, he fell down. I took this moment and grabbed more shopping carts. I backed them into the entrance and exit doors.

He got up and began pounding on the glass. I could see the other figures off in the distance coming this way as well.

I continued grabbing carts and created a barricade against the door so no one else could get in.

While doing so, my blood spilled all over them. He'd taken a good clean chunk out of me and I began feeling a little dizzy. I struggled to get the carts up against the doors before I would retreat back to the registers to check on Linda.

After a few moments, I did just that. However, when I got to the registers, I found a pool of blood, the deceased customer, but no Linda. She was nowhere to be found.

I tried to call out to her but couldn't find my voice. The store's surroundings got blurry and…

JOEY

I was surrounded. I was only blocks away from getting to Georgio's, but there was no way I could get through the crowd. I took off, leaving my car and accidentally dropping my cell phone. This virus was completely out of control and I didn't want to get near anyone infected with it.

So I ran. I just kept running, not sure where to go.

Hours passed and I found myself hiding out near a gas station. I was in the alleyway, crouching behind a dumpster, as sick people moved around me. Some guys on motorcycles even drove by, shooting at them. I saw at least three people get shot. I couldn't believe it. I realized that I didn't want to be found by anyone right now—not the sick people, and not the bikers.

After they'd passed by and the area was relatively deserted, I tried my best to scope out the gas station without being spotted by anyone.

Tara kept crossing my mind, and I prayed that she stayed put. I had every intention of getting over to the restaurant despite my current detour. As I snuck out of the alley, I noticed someone nearby.

I had no way of knowing if this person was healthy or even if they were sane, but it seemed like my best chance. So, I started heading out of the alley.

All of a sudden, I ran right into a sick person. We fell to the ground and she rolled on top of me.

"Oh gosh," I said, "I'm so sorry."

She made a gurgling sound, opened her mouth wide, and leaned forward to bite my neck. I wasn't sure what her intentions were, but I didn't want to find out, so I pushed her off me. Then, I got to my feet as she did the same.

"Take it easy," I said.

She looked at me with vacant eyes and curled her discolored lips over her teeth, moaning at me.

Then, a loud bang came from behind me and her head exploded! I nearly fell at the sound of the shot. I looked behind me and saw an Indian (from India not the other kind) man in a gas station uniform holding a shotgun.

"Come on," he said. "Let's get inside before more show up!"

I followed the man into the gas station, shocked at what I had just witnessed.

This man had just blown someone's head clean off. I was in shock, but the gravity of the situation was slowly sinking in as I followed him without question.

"Get away from the door," he said and locked it behind us.

I moved to the back of the store. He approached me, holding the shotgun in one hand and looking for a handshake with the other, "I'm Hamin," he said.

Reluctantly, I shook his hand, "Joey. Nice to meet you."

He nodded and put the gun down. Most of the lights were off in the store and he simply sat down behind the counter. "Don't move around too much," he said.

I nodded. "I have to get to Georgio's Pizzeria."

"If you're hungry, help yourself," he smirked.

"No, no, I have to find someone."

"Sorry, friend, you're on your own there."

"What's going on exactly? Why did you shoot that girl? I know she was sick, but why?"

"They go down with headshots," he said.

I continued to listen, even though I was confused as hell.

Hamin didn't tell me much. He just explained what he knew; the infection spreads through the blood—bites or scratches, and the only way to take down an infected person was to destroy the brain. I felt like I was taking part in some sort of new reality TV show—none of it seemed like it could be real.

He told me I should at least wait until morning to head out. That he would give me a car to use from his garage. So I waited with him. We didn't talk much after that. We each spent some time reading magazines and keeping an eye on what was happening outside.

He had a radio so we listed to that too. People stumbled by in groups of three or four for the most part. Every now and then, we noticed one person alone coming down the street. One man came into the gas station parking lot and walked over the bell cord.

When the bell went off, the man went crazy. He started looking around and kind of shouting to himself. In his confusion, he stepped on the bell two more times. It was almost funny to see him so confused, but it was also tough to watch. I couldn't comprehend a human acting so primitively.

"I might have to get rid of him," Hamin said. "Before he brings more here."

Ding. Ding.

The confused man stepped on the bell a couple more times.

"Okay, stay by the door," Hamin ordered before he went outside.

I held the door closed as he slowly approached the man outside. He looked back at me and then raised his shotgun. Quickly and swiftly, he pulled the trigger and blasted a hole through the diseased man's skull. The corpse fell to the ground.

Ding.

It landed directly on the cord. Hamin inspected the corpse for a moment before turning back to me. As he turned around, he spotted three other infected people moving toward him.

"Shit, they see me," he said.

I opened the door a crack and yelled, "Get back in here!"

"No, they'll only pile up against the door," he said.

"Shit," I said as I closed the door.

Hamin moved towards them at an awkward angle. After a moment, I realized he was drawing them away from the gas pumps. Given our current predicament, I could understand him not wanting to deal with a massive explosion.

The number of infected grew by a few more as a handful of them continued coming into the gas station's parking lot. I couldn't make out exactly what Hamin was saying, but I thought I heard him say something along the lines of, "I should've brought more shells!"

I glanced around to see if there was a box of shells somewhere, but I didn't see any. So I stayed at the door, not knowing what else to do.

Hamin continued to move swiftly around the gas pumps, baiting the people and getting them to go where he wanted. He was good at it, and it made me wonder a little bit about his past.

Soon, he was able to get them together and he took his first shot at the group. He shot two of them in the head and both bodies fell to the ground, limp. Needless to say, I was impressed.

Then he started to run back to me. He stopped by the air pump off to the side and pulled a couple of shells from his pocket and reloaded the shotgun. I turned away and watched as four more infected moved past the pumps, closer to Hamin and me.

His shotgun went off again and it startled me. I turned back to him and saw him stumbling backwards as another sick person he hadn't seen moved toward him. This one must've snuck up on Hamin.

He fired a shot and hit the infected man right between the eyes.

"Shit!" he yelled as he turned back toward me. His arm was bleeding and it appeared he'd been bitten or scratched. He ran to the door and tossed the shotgun on the ground. I went to open the door but he said, "I'm out of shells and I'm bit. Keep it shut until they're gone!"

He ran past the door and starting shouting to the infected people. "Hey! Come on! Over here, I've got something for you! It's dinner time!"

I looked on in amazement as he ran into the road and stood there. Most of the infected followed him like fish after a worm. But two others noticed me at the door. They immediately were fixated on me.

I looked at the shotgun on the ground outside and decided I couldn't get it in time, so I quickly locked the door and ran behind the counter to stay out of sight.

I heard Hamin scream, and when I peeked outside, I saw he hadn't escaped his pursuers. They had surrounded him and closed the circle.

The two infected were pounding on the door while the rest tore Hamin apart. There was barely anything left in the road by the time they were through.

After they were done feasting, they headed my way. They couldn't see me in the dark behind the counter, but I could see them. They were hungry and covered in blood. Pounding on the door and the building, there was nothing I could do but wait. I didn't know if the back exit was accessible, and I was so scared I didn't consider it an option.

I was trapped for the time being. So I sat and I waited.

Days turned into weeks as I hunkered down in the gas station, feeding on snack foods: Trail mix, candy, chips, power bars, sodas, sports drinks and bottled waters. The damn radio broke and I couldn't get it to work.

I read every magazine available and even considered scratching the scratch tickets for the fun of it.

I tried to remain hidden and not call attention to myself. Tara crossed my mind from time to time. I dreaded the thought of her out there, in the street, as one of those *things*.

Then, one day some people showed up. I watched them get gas. One of them tried to open the door and was apparently so desperate that he smashed the glass to get in. When they left, I followed them.

FROM THE FILES OF DOCTOR JOANNE SANDERS

On the night of June thirteenth, Massachusetts General Hospital was forced to lock their doors, turning away nearly one hundred people seeking medical assistance. At this point in time, we were overrun with Arthriphagy carriers. More than fifty percent of the hospital grounds had been designated as quarantine zones.

By the time this happened, our numbers had increased by over a hundred. Seventy-seven patients had succumbed to the virus. During treatment, thirty members of our staff were also infected and since have been quarantined. Prior to these zones being established, three patients had to be euthanized. We remain now with a hundred and four 'A.Phagy' carriers locked in the quarantined areas.

Seventeen other staff members have remained in the hospital, running tests and/or simply waiting it out. I've taken fifty-two blood samples from people at different stages of infection. These samples are to be replicated and further testing will be done. So far, I've confirmed that all fifty-two samples have tested positive for Arthriphagy.

Helicopters had been called for pick-up of essential staff members. We were told that we'd be going to New Hampshire and relocated to a safe zone there. When the helicopters arrived and each picked up eight staff members, I was given a message to wait on the roof with my samples and any Arthriphagy related research I'd obtained.

Moments later, another helicopter — this one entirely black — landed. A man dressed in a suit came out to greet me. He told me that we'd be going to the Center for Disease Control (CDC) in Atlanta, Georgia.

I boarded the transport and was introduced to Dr. Phillip Woodson, head of the Arthriphagy Research Team (ART).

He informed me that my samples and work thus far showed great potential and that I'd be leading a division of ART at the CDC.

Upon arrival to the CDC, I was assigned to a branch of the building and introduced to a dozen lab technicians who were assigned with the task of replicating all fifty-two samples.

Research for a cure and treatment of the Arthriphagy virus is set to begin immediately.

Dr. J. Sanders

ZOMBIE BUFFET: AN UNDEAD ANTHOLOGY

Edited by Anthony Giangregorio

If you're hungry for zombie stories, look no further than this anthology.

There's enough rotting meat to satisfy even the most discerning connoisseur, and our all-you-can-eat buffet is sure to please.

Rotting intestines, severed heads and exploding spleens are just some of the courses waiting for you within this book of undead mastication.

So grab a knife and fork, slap on a napkin, 'cause you're gonna get dirty, and prepare yourself for the Zombie Buffet.

A zombie feast of epic proportions.

DEAD CHRISTMAS: A ZOMBIE ANTHOLOGY

Edited by Anthony Giangregorio

Share the most special time of the year with someone you love, or better yet, with an animated corpse!

The living dead love Christmas. Whether they're hanging their entrails like garland, using severed heads like stockings, or hanging body parts like ornaments, even zombies enjoy the most wonderful time of the year.

Santa Claus isn't immune to the walking dead, either.

Zombie elves, killer reindeer and undead hordes, all seek to share in the joy of the holiday . . . and tear Santa apart and feed on his flesh.

So when you grab last year's fruitcake to re-gift to Aunt Martha, just make sure to bring a shotgun, too. Because for all you know, your aunt has turned into an undead flesh-eater, and if the shotgun won't kill her, the fruitcake most assuredly will.

RATS

By Anthony Giangregorio

Killer black rats the size of dogs are roaming the streets and no one is aware of their existence.

Wild dogs, the authorities warn. Stay indoors and all will be fine.

Domenic Salvatore soon finds himself in the middle of a cover-up of epic proportions; where no one will believe the truth.

And why would they? After all, he's just a kid.

What no one knows is that the rats have taken on a taste for human meat, a particular kind of meat actually…young flesh…the flesh of children.

As the kids are hunted one by one, killed and dragged off into the night to be devoured, Domenic realizes that it's only a matter of time before he's next.

Something evil stalks the town of Wakefield, Mass…and it's hungry.

BIGFOOT TALES

Edited by Mark Christopher

The elusive Bigfoot has been a mystery for years.

Truth or hoax? No one knows for sure and perhaps never will.

So does this creature of the forest truly exist? Is there really a missing link that ties together man with his ape ancestors?

Or is it all simply a figment of the imagination.

CLAN OF THE BIGFOOT

ANTHONY GIANGREGORIO

ZOMBIES, MONSTERS, CREATURES OF THE NIGHT

OPEN CASKET PRESS

OPEN CASKET PRESS.COM
THE NEW NAME IN HORROR

THE PLACE TO GO FOR ZOMBIE AND APOCALYPTIC FICTION

 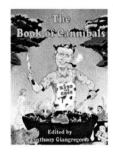 

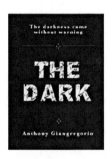  

LIVING DEAD PRESS

WHERE THE DEAD WALK
www.livingdeadpress.com